Pn

D1343934

ANIMAL INSTINCTS

When Jemma's new boss Matt suggests bringing a TV crew into the wildlife park, she reluctantly agrees. As Head of Mammals, she's occupied with the animals — and most urgently, the attempt to get their two giant pandas to breed. But the demanding TV director is more interested in another relationship and, at his insistence, Jemma and Matt find themselves acting out an on-screen romance. Despite Jemma's best attempts to resist the feelings that are surfacing, could it be that the blossoming romance is not just for the cameras?

SARAH PURDUE

ANIMAL INSTINCTS

Complete and Unabridged

LINFORD
Leicester

First published in Great Britain in 2019

First Linford Edition
published 2020

A catalogue record for this book is available
from the British Library.

ISBN 978–1–4448–4431–3

Published by
Ulverscroft Limited
Anstey, Leicestershire

Set by Words & Graphics Ltd.
Anstey, Leicestershire
Printed and bound in Great Britain by
T. J. International Ltd., Padstow, Cornwall

This book is printed on acid-free paper

No Love Lost

'If I can have your attention, people?' the man in the grey, three-piece suit, shiny black patent shoes and expensive haircut, said. The crowd didn't show any signs of quietening, so the man held his hands up as if he were thanking them for their adoration. This seemed to stun the crowd into temporary silence.

'I know that many of you are worried about the changes that we have instigated since taking over the management of the zoo.'

'It's a wildlife park, or at least it was,' Ted murmured. He was wearing stained overalls and stood at the back of the room. The rest of the room, bar the man in the sharp suit, rumbled their agreement.

'As I said, we of the new management group acknowledge your concerns and we have listened carefully to all your comments.'

The room as one raised an eyebrow at such an obviously spurious statement.

'But the fact remains that in order to provide the best care for our animals we need to make money and so I would urge you to embrace the changes and walk with us into this new chapter.'

The man in the suit brought his hands together as if he was expecting a rousing round of applause, but he was met with stony silence.

'Well, those animals won't feed themselves,' he said, his positive, upbeat tone slipping just a little, 'and I must be getting on.' And with that, he scurried away.

'I can't believe this is happening,' Ted said, looking miserably at the artist's impressions of their new uniforms, which lined the walls of the wildlife park restaurant. 'What's wrong with what we've always worn?'

Jemma looked Ted up and down. She was sure that Mrs Ted probably insisted on washing his uniform but, since Ted worked with primates who were notoriously messy, it was clear that standard washing powder made no impact on the stains and general odour.

'You've had those for years, Ted. Probably time you had a new set of overalls.'

'Aye, but I'm not getting overalls, am I?' Ted said, jabbing at the poster on the wall which had the new primate team uniform.

'I'm getting a monkey suit.'

Jemma's eyes strayed from Ted's face to the uniform picture. He wasn't far wrong. The new uniform consisted of a brown baseball cap with furry mock monkey ears, a T-shirt that had a stylised monkey logo on the front and back, and a pair of cargo trousers, which came complete with a monkey tail attached to the back seam.

'Mr Darnell seems to think it will make us more approachable to the visitors.'

'Mr Darnell wants to dress up like

this and step in with the lemurs. They're going to go nuts and you know they'll be permanently trying to pinch me tail,' Ted said gloomily.

Jemma gave him a reassuring pat on the back.

'If it brings more visitors we can probably move forward with improving the habitats,' Jemma said, trying to sound positive although she felt anything but. Being Head of Mammals hadn't saved her from the new uniform either. Hers was similar to Ted's and the other primate keepers, except she would be dressed to look like a giant panda, all black and white, with a furry cap with ears. At least she didn't have a dangling tail, she supposed.

'Is that before or after he's paid out a fortune for our new uniforms?' Ted said the words as if they were in inverted commas.

'We have to make it work,' Jemma said, now much more serious. 'It's this or we have to find new homes for all our animals.'

'Aye,' Ted said miserably before following the others out of the open double doors and into the park.

Jemma watched as they all dispersed to their duties. Tomorrow they would all be decked out in their new outfits but today at least they looked like proper keepers and not teenagers employed by the nearby theme park, which Mr Darnell had also recently purchased — another family business taken over by big business and whose employers only seemed interested in how much money they could make.

Still, it was better than having to find new homes for the animals, some of which the keepers had been caring for for decades, and that was before she considered how difficult it would be for all her staff to find new work.

No, they had to make the best of it and if it meant wearing ridiculous uniforms then that's what they would have to do.

Jemma followed her well-worn trail, which she took every morning, to check in on each of the animal enclosures that formed the large mammal section of the park.

She walked passed the lions who were sunbathing as if they had no cares in the world, and passed the snow leopards who sat high in the branches of their favourite tree, flicking their tails.

She turned the corner and found herself outside the large enclosure which was home to what Mr Darnell had described as the zoo's 'main feature' — the two giant pandas.

Since it was the end of April, this was panda breeding season but so far Bojing and Lijuan had given the impression of being exes who couldn't stand the sight of each other.

Looking into the enclosure she could see that the pandas were sitting as far apart as possible, with their backs to each other. Not a promising sight. Rosie, the head keeper for the pandas, had piled up the bamboo in the no-panda zone in the middle of the enclosure, in an effort to entice them to at least look at each other but it seemed that they would only approach the pile when they were sure the other one wasn't looking.

'What we need is to make Bojing look more attractive,' Rosie said, walking up beside her.

'I'm open to ideas,' Jemma said, who had undertaken extensive research but had so far not come up with anything which had encouraged the two to tolerate each other's presence, let alone fall in love.

'I think we need to make him look more manly,' Rosie said, her eyes fixed on Bojing, who was now lying on his back and chewing on a bamboo shoot as if he had no troubles in the world.

Jemma raised an eyebrow. Rosie's ideas had become wackier the more desperate they had all got, as the breeding season was heading to a close for another year.

'Maybe we need to get another male,' a voice said behind them and they both turned around. The park wasn't open yet, so they knew it wasn't a member of the public. The tall, broad shouldered man was wearing a suit and that could mean only one thing — he was part of the new management team.

'Matt Darnell,' he said, holding out a hand to each of them in turn.

'Any relation to Mr Darnell?' Rosie said, and her voice had gone all high and giggly, as her eyes checked out the new man on the scene.

'He's my uncle but don't hold that against me.' Matt smiled and it was a cheerful kind of smile but Jemma didn't feel like smiling back. Right now, she didn't need another man in a suit, whose only concern was the park's profit margin, making foolish suggestions like simply going out and getting another panda, as if they could be bought online for a small fee.

'Mr Darnell . . . ' Jemma started to say.

'Please, call me Matt,' he said with another smile, which didn't falter even when Jemma didn't smile back.

'Matt, the panda is an endangered species, which is one of the reasons why we have them here. I'm afraid it is not possible to simply go out and buy another one. For one thing, as you can imagine, the Chinese are notoriously protective of this species.'

Jemma knew her voice was icy, the kind of tone that she reserved for people that mistreated animals, and that it was probably undeserved, but she couldn't help herself.

'Of course, I understand,' he said. 'I just wondered if some competition might up his game? You know that tends to work for humans.'

Rosie giggled and Jemma glared at her.

'We could always dress up as bears and see if that works,' Rosie said, barely being able to get the words out between her high-pitched bouts of laughter.

'Go for it,' Matt said. 'Babies are always good for getting in the visitors and baby pandas would bring them in from far and wide.'

He grinned once more, and Jemma knew that he was completely aware of the impact that he had on Rosie. He winked at Rosie who covered her mouth and giggled some more.

'I'm in the office, ladies, if you need anything. Jemma, perhaps you could find time in your busy schedule to pop up and see me sometime? Shall we say tomorrow morning?'

Rosie stood, mouth open, as he strode away but all Jemma could do was glare at his retreating back, thinking that the last thing they needed right now was another man in a suit suggesting that the answer might be dressing up in ridiculous costumes.

The Craziness Begins

Jemma knocked on the door and waited. It wasn't lost on her that the management offices seemed to have had an full scale refurbishment.

Interesting — since she had recently been told the clipboards they used for documenting the well-being of each of their animals couldn't be replaced due to limited funds, even if some of them had been chewed by members of the rodent display and one had been stolen by the family of monkeys.

Despite all this, Jemma had been told they would have to 'make do', but there didn't seem to be much of that happening in the management offices.

'Come in,' the voice said, and Jemma took a deep breath before pushing open the door. She had taken off her furry panda hat but was still decked out in her black and white camouflage uniform that made her look only slightly less ridiculous than the primate team.

She had wondered if the years of her life spent studying animal behaviour and welfare at university had been worth it. Certainly, if someone had told her she would have to dress like this every day she might have considered a career at Disneyland. At least they had better costumes.

'Mr Darnell,' Jemma said before taking the chair that he indicated with a wave of his hand.

'Really, Jemma, please call me Matt. I'm not my uncle.'

Jemma personally thought he was doing well at being a junior version of his uncle, but she kept her mouth closed. There was a lot at stake and she needed to remain professional, however challenging it was to deal with people like the Darnells.

'What did you want to see me about, Matt?' Jemma said, making sure to put suitable emphasis on the use of his first name.

Matt grinned and looked a tad triumphant, as though he had achieved his goal for the day and Jemma had to blink so as not to roll her eyes.

'I wanted a panda update,' Matt said, still smiling.

'Both Bojing and Lijuan are in good health.'

'Indeed, which is fantastic news. We can all agree on that, but what I really want to know is when we can expect the pitter-patter of tiny paws.'

'I think we would all like to know that,' Jemma said and then cleared her throat before reminding herself who she was talking to. 'Breeding in captivity is difficult. You can't simply introduce two members of the same species and expect babies to follow.'

'The other departments don't seem to have that problem. In fact, we have some issues with increased numbers in the reptile centre.'

'Reptiles, I am led to believe, are a bit like rabbits. Unfortunately, pandas are not.'

Matt leaned back in his brand new, black leather executive chair and steepled his fingers.

'If they were, every zoo would have baby pandas bounding around,' Jemma added for good measure.

Matt nodded thoughtfully.

'There is one place where they have good success rates.'

Now Jemma nodded. In China, where pandas originated from, they had successful breeding programmes, but they were also able to reproduce the climate and surroundings that were closer to their natural habitat and that was before you dealt with the bamboo issue, which grew naturally in China and was much harder to come by in Britain.

'Perhaps we can arrange to speak with some of those experts?'

Jemma tried not to show her emotions on her face. After all, she was a well-respected expert in the field and had spent some time in China, studying bears in their natural habitat, but Matt seemed oblivious to this fact.

'Well, I have friends and colleagues in China and around the world, whom I speak to on a regular basis, where we share expertise and ideas.'

Matt nodded but Jemma saw something shift a little on his face. She didn't know him well but she sensed she had made him uncomfortable.

'Was there anything else?' Jemma raised one eyebrow and wondered what vital piece of equipment they were going to have to live without this time. Judging by the look on Matt's face, there was bad news to come.

'Yes, there is, actually, and I think it's something that we can all get behind.'

Jemma suspected it was going to be exactly the kind of thing that she wouldn't want to get behind.

'We have been approached by a wildlife documentary crew who would like to film at the zoo.'

Jemma digested this information and nodded. That might not be so bad. After all, if they could get the park featured on TV maybe more people would come and visit, which would improve the chances of the park staying open and the much loved animals staying put.

'OK, I think we can probably cope with that,' Jemma said out loud. 'It could help raise the profile of the park as well.'

'My thoughts exactly,' Matt said, leaning forward and the excitement showing on his face.

Jemma had to bite her lip to keep from smiling. He was like a little boy in a toy shop and it was kind of endearing. As soon as the thought arrived, she pushed it away. The last thing she needed was to go all slushy over the new owner's nephew.

'They want to call the documentary 'Panda-monium',' Matt said, making a rainbow action with his hands, much like an old time Hollywood director.

Jemma mouthed the word 'Panda-monium' and any hope that had come with the news quickly faded. It sounded more like bad reality TV than a serious wildlife documentary.

'They want it to be fly-on-the-wall stuff. So, they intend to follow you and your staff around twenty-four seven and then they will cut together the good stuff.'

Jemma's heart sank even further. She could just picture the chaos and disruption that would occur once certain members of her team found out they were going to be followed by cameras through every aspect of their duties.

In her mind's eye she could picture heavy make-up and shoving to get the best camera angles. She was going to have to sit them down for a serious chat and then be an eagle-eyed presence. It was the last thing she needed but one look at Matt's face told her that this would be non-negotiable.

'Right,' Jemma said, trying to sound upbeat about the prospect of having her every move recorded by a TV crew. 'When do they start?'

'They want to start filming tomorrow afternoon and so the crew will be getting settled in the morning.'

That didn't give her much time to get her team in order, but it would have to do. Jemma nodded.

'I'll go and brief my team.' Jemma stood up but something about Matt's expression made her think that he wasn't ready for her to leave. 'Unless there was something else?'

'There was, actually.'

Jemma made no move to sit down. She didn't really have time for this and when Matt realised that she wasn't going to, he cleared his throat and continued.

'I wondered if you would join me for dinner this evening?'

Jemma froze, feeling like she had just been asked to the school disco by the one person she didn't want to ask her. Her expression must have been all too clear to Matt.

'For a strategy meeting, of course,' he quickly added. 'I figured you wouldn't have time today to sit down with me and if I'm going to take up your evening the least thing I can do is ensure you get something to eat.'

Jemma nodded, feeling completely wrong footed. Had she misread the original suggestion? It had sounded like he was asking her out but now he looked as though he felt sorry for her, that she had somehow got the wrong idea about his suggestion.

'Of course, that would be fine,' Jemma mumbled, wishing she was anywhere but here. She had a PhD in animal behaviour, how had she misread his body language? It was most unsettling.

'Would the pub in the village suit?' Matt asked.

'That would be fine,' Jemma said faintly, still trying to work out what had just happened.

'Shall we say seven?'

Jemma nodded, not trusting herself to say anything else. Matt smiled and then his eyes strayed to a pile of paperwork on his desk, which Jemma took as a sign that she was dismissed.

She left the office and walked out of the building, her mind reeling with what had just happened. She was an expert in reading between the lines and identifying behaviour, that was her thing, so why was it failing her so badly now? She was still lost in that thought when she found herself back near the panda enclosure.

'What did Mr Dreamboat want?' Rosie asked, appearing from the keeper area of the enclosure and moving to stand next to Jemma, who was now staring at the two pandas.

The bears were sitting with their backs to each other and, as had become the norm, were as far apart as they could possibly be.

'Hmm?' Jemma realised that Rosie was talking to her but had no idea what she had just said. Rosie's giggle brought her back to the present and she could see her eyes were sparkling with mischief.

'I knew it!' Rosie said triumphantly.

Jemma decided to head her off before she could get too carried away.

'He wanted to tell me that we have a

film crew coming to make a documentary about us.'

Jemma's words had the desired effect as Rosie's eyes went wide and her mouth formed a perfect 'O'.

'When?' Rosie squeaked.

'First thing tomorrow morning.' Jemma watched as Rosie's hands went to her hair and she knew what was coming next.

'I need the afternoon off!' Rosie squeaked. 'I can't be on the telly with my hair looking like this.'

Jemma sighed. The craziness had already begun.

Too Late to Escape

Jemma walked through the door to her flat at ten minutes to seven but since it wasn't a date she saw no reason to rush. If she was late it was because she had been working getting everything in place for the filming that was due to start the next day, and since that was Matt's directive she had no intention of apologising for her tardiness.

She hopped in the shower and then dressed in jeans and a T-shirt. Jemma checked her appearance in the mirror that hung on the back of her bedroom door and nodded her approval. She looked exactly like someone who had rushed home from work and didn't have the time or inclination to make more of an effort.

Pushing open the door to the local pub, Jemma saw plenty of people that she recognised. The village was small, and they only had one pub, so that was not much of a surprise. She waved at a few people and scanned the room for sign of Matt.

She spotted him easily, since he was the only person in the pub who had dressed up. He was wearing navy blue chinos, a white short-sleeved shirt and had a jumper slung around his shoulders.

He looked more ready for a day at Henley regatta than a working dinner with a subordinate.

Jemma's mind immediately went to the place she was desperately trying to avoid. His attire screamed 'date' but she forced herself to imagine what Matt would wear to a works dinner and her mind's eye pictured him as he was.

He did after all wear a three-piece suit to work, in an animal wildlife park, so naturally he would assume that this appropriate dress for the local pub. Matt looked up and waved a hand in Jemma's direction.

Jemma could feel the eyes of

everyone in the pub follow her to Matt's table. Most of the people there had some connection with the park, whether they worked there in some capacity or worked for a local business that supplied the park, so everyone knew exactly who Matt was.

And it seemed everyone was curious as to why Jemma was meeting him in the pub.

Jemma could only imagine what they were thinking but forced the thoughts from her mind. Instead, she strode over and held out a hand. This caught Matt by surprise, but he was quickly on his feet and returning the gesture.

'Mr Darnell, I'm sorry I'm late but I was busy at work putting the final preparations in place for our visitors tomorrow.' Jemma's voice was louder than strictly necessary, but a quick glance told her the rest of the pub had heard her words and for now, at least, they seemed content to go back to whatever they had been discussing before her entrance.

Matt nodded, and Jemma was sure he had understood what had just happened, but thankfully he didn't seem to feel the need to comment.

'Shall we order? Then we can get on with business. I appreciate that you've had a long day and what with the early start tomorrow I think it would be good to wrap this up quickly.'

Jemma stared. Matt seemed to be talking loudly enough for the rest of the pub to hear, too. Did he feel the same as her? Not wanting to give the impression that this was anything but a business meeting that happened to include some food? Somehow the thought that he felt like that annoyed her and she wasn't entirely sure why.

'What will it be, pet?' Maggie asked, 'Your usual?'

'Please,' Jemma said with a smile.

'And you, Mr Darnell?' Maggie asked.

'Please, call me Matt,' Matt said, switching on his winning smile. Jemma was just trying to hide a smirk at the idea that Matt's charm might work on Maggie, when Maggie giggled.

Jemma's eyes went wide. She couldn't help it. Charm just didn't work on Maggie who was far too much of a straight talker for all of that nonsense but here she was giggling like a school girl. Now Jemma was sure that the world was going mad.

'Well, then, Matt,' Maggie said, putting plenty of emphasis on his name, 'what can I get you this fine evening?'

'Hmm,' Matt said studying the menu. 'What do you recommend?'

'My home-made steak and kidney pud is fairly popular,' Maggie said, smiling sweetly down at him. Jemma had to look away, it was all too much.

'Home-made? Well, how could I possibly resist?'

Jemma made a decision in that moment that she was never going to be overcome by the force of his charm. She knew she would need to be strong but there was no way she wanted to turn into a giggling teenager.

There were too many other important things to be dealing with right now. Maggie sashayed away, and Matt's attention fell back to Jemma, who had time to rearrange her face to a polite expression.

'So, tomorrow . . . ' she prompted.

Matt rubbed his hands together. 'Tomorrow. The film crew will be on site at half seven. They want to scout out the various locations before they start filming. They'll be getting some background shots of the zoo . . . '

'Wildlife park,' Jemma said automatically.

Matt looked at her quizzically and then shrugged.

'Wildlife park,' he said slowly. 'Then they are going to do an interview with you so that you can provide an introduction to the bears and the current status quo.'

Jemma started to nod and then realised what Matt had just said.

'Wait a second, they want to interview me, on camera?'

'Well, yes. I know that Rosie is head keeper, but you are the resident expert.'

Jemma could feel her insides wince, she had walked right into that one. At least he had listened to her and maybe even looked at her personnel file?

She had of course considered that she might be caught on film, but she hadn't really thought that they would want to interview her. Unlike the rest of her team, she didn't have a lifelong dream of her fifteen minutes of fame.

'Since I arranged the visit, I thought it was only right that I will be there with you to greet the crew,' Matt said, seemingly oblivious to the internal battle that was raging through Jemma's mind.

Maggie arrived with their dinners and placed them on the table, winking at Matt before she left.

Jemma closed her eyes and swallowed. This would be good publicity for the park, which would generate more income and in turn that would benefit the animals and that was all that mattered. She would give her interview and then do her best to stay off stage. How bad could it be?

'So is the TV crew from the BBC?' Jemma asked, feeling like she needed to focus on something other than her own upcoming appearance.

'Not exactly,' Matt said and he at least had the decency to look a little sheepish.

Jemma stared, she couldn't help it. What on earth had Matt got them in to? Just who was coming to film the documentary?

'Not exactly?' Jemma repeated but already she could feel the dread work up through her until her heart sank.

'They're a new production company.'

'Oh, yes?' Jemma said. She would have naturally preferred an experienced crew, but it might not be so bad. She at least might have a bit more say in what and when they filmed. 'No previous experience, then?' she asked since it looked as if Matt had lost the power of speech.

'First wildlife feature,' Matt admitted, staring at his steak and kidney pud in a way that suggested he wished the conversation was over.

'But they've made other television?' Jemma asked. There was clearly something Matt wasn't telling her and she needed to know what it was.

'You could argue that they have had previous experience with unpredictable subjects.' Matt now flashed her a slightly uncertain grin and Jemma felt like she was getting a migraine.

She closed her eyes briefly and then fixed Matt with a stern look, one that said she was done with dancing around the issue and he needed to just come right out and tell her.

'They made a kind of fly-on-the-wall documentary about the horribly rich.'

Jemma was about to eat a chip but found herself frozen in time. She wasn't much of a TV watcher herself but she did listen to the rest of her team, some of whom were avid reality TV show fans.

Jemma had a feeling she knew exactly the programme Matt was referring to. She had watched five minutes of it once, on the insistence of Rosie, but had found it unbearable. It was ghastly and sensational, and the TV crew seemed to be ever present, in every aspect of the badly behaved lives of the subjects.

'Not 'Filthy Rich'?' Jemma squeaked.

'Look, it won't be as bad as all that . . . ' Matt started to say but Jemma just stared at him incredulously and he stopped talking.

'Have you ever watched it? It's dreadful!'

'No, I haven't,' Matt said, 'and I'll admit that I'm surprised you have.'

Jemma felt her cheeks colour.

'I watched five minutes of it, to see what all the fuss was about and then promised myself never again.'

'I understand your concerns,' Matt said holding up two hands, 'but I have spoken at length to the director. They want to take the company in a new direction — a much more serious direction — and it seemed like the perfect match.'

Jemma knew that if she read between the lines, it was likely that the production company had offered the park a generous subsidy for being on the premises.

Jemma felt like she was waving goodbye to her hard-earned reputation and for the first time in her life wondered if her sister had been right, and that she should have become an accountant.

Matt had continued to talk but Jemma had found it hard to pay attention to his words. She had spent her time desperately trying to figure out a way to stop the disaster before it happened, but she had come up with nothing.

'Great, so we're in agreement.'

Jemma forced herself to focus on Matt's face but was momentarily distracted by his warm brown eyes. She blinked and mentally made an effort to pull herself together.

'I'm sorry . . . what did you say?' she asked to give herself more time to work out what was going on.

'I said, I'm glad we agree. This will be so much more straightforward if we are both on the same page.'

'Absolutely,' Jemma said, still with no idea what she had just agreed to.

'Fantastic,' Matt said, looking at the expensive watch on his wrist. 'Now if you'll excuse me, Betty gets upset if I'm later than I say I'll be.' And he stood up, placing some crisp notes on to the table. 'I'll see you at work? I think it would be good to meet at around ten? Then we can discuss the day's filming with the director.'

Jemma nodded, feeling like she had lost the power of speech. She should have been thinking about the film crew, about reducing the damage to the wildlife park and her reputation but all she could think about was who Betty was. By the time she had shaken herself and firmly told herself to focus, Matt was gone.

CUT!

Jemma kept hoping that she was trapped in a nightmare and that any minute she would wake up, but despite pinching herself, she remained resolutely present.

The wildlife park had been taken over by the film crew — quite a task considering how many acres it covered. Everywhere you looked there were generators, belching out noise and smoke. Cables, literally miles of cables, were trailed all across the ground, around every enclosure.

Jemma had to insist that they move the cables when one of the squirrel monkeys had managed to grab a stray cable and pull it into his enclosure, before setting to work on it with his tiny teeth.

At ten o'clock, Matt finally appeared, looking as fresh as a daisy in comparison to Jemma, who was wearing a fake fur cap in 25-degree heat.

'Right, then. The director has the crew all set, so they are ready for you to do your first interview.'

'I was planning to change out of my uniform into something more suitable,' Jemma said.

'Ah, no, I'm afraid that's not possible.'

'Oh?' Jemma said, raising an eyebrow and wondering if it was worth fighting Matt over. At this stage, she doubted that wearing a furry cap designed to make her look like a panda could actually make the day any worse.

'The director was insistent that you wear the uniform. He thinks it will play well on camera and you know, make it clear to the viewer who you are.'

'Couldn't he just introduce me or put one of those tags on the bottom of the screen?'

'I'm not sure it's that kind of documentary,' Matt said, 'and it's not the sort of thing that you see on a David Attenborough, is it?'

Jemma sighed and shrugged. David

Attenborough? They should be so lucky! She followed Matt to the small conference room that had been set up to work as a TV studio. In one corner was a stool, set up in front of a green screen.

Jemma could only imagine what they were going to super-impose her image over. She wondered if she could fake some kind of animal related emergency to get out of filming the interview.

'Jemma, I would like to introduce Johnny Beckett, the director of the documentary.'

Jemma forced her mind away from escape routes and on to the man standing in front of her. He was dressed as if he was heading out into the jungle, the real jungle — if the real jungle meant you needed to wear long pale socks, with open-toed sandals and a hunter's hat. He looked ridiculous and did nothing to buoy Jemma's hopes.

Johnny Beckett was holding out his hand and so Jemma shook it and tried not to look horrified.

'Jemma, darling, you absolutely look the part,' he said as if he were genuinely delighted by her panda uniform.

'New uniforms,' was all that Jemma could think of to say.

'Yes, well you look fabulous and they should really liven things up.'

Jemma nodded, in the way you do when you know you are supposed to agree but really don't. Personally, she still felt like she was working at a holiday camp. She took off her hat, thinking that would reduce the slightly lunatic impression she thought she was giving.

'Take a seat, Jemma — and hat on, please!' Johnny announced, clapping his hands at the rest of his crew who seemed to suddenly come alive and rush around pressing buttons.

Jemma sat on the stool and tried not to stare at the camera. She felt like a rabbit in the headlights, especially since all the room seemed focused on her.

'So, Jemma,' Director Johnny said, 'When did you first develop your passion for pandas?'

Jemma stared at him. What an odd way to put things. She shook herself a little and tried to focus on the question.

'I've always been passionate about animals and their well-being . . . ' Jemma started to say but didn't get any further as Johnny yelled 'CUT!' so loudly that she nearly fell off her stool.

'Jemma, darling, we don't want to bore the viewers with your life story. Perhaps you could just cut to the bit where you decide that pandas are your thing.'

Jemma risked a glance at Matt, hoping that he might step in and rescue her but Matt just smiled encouragingly, as if everything were OK.

'Whilst studying for my PhD in animal behaviour and welfare I was able to travel to China and work as part of the panda breeding programme.' Jemma paused, Johnny didn't exactly look enthused but since he hadn't yelled, 'Cut!' she figured she should just keep going.

'Pandas are difficult to breed in captivity and I was able to gain many invaluable insights whilst working with the local experts.' Jemma paused again as Johnny ran a hand through his seriously receding hairline.

'She's not exactly a natural,' Johnny said, ignoring Jemma and turning to Matt.

'Jemma is our resident expert,' Matt said and Jemma felt a little glow inside that Matt was defending her, 'but she has never been on film before. I'm sure she'll improve with experience.' Jemma felt the glow go out as if a bucket of cold water had just been thrown over it.

'Perhaps you would be better suited to giving an interview?' Jemma asked, keeping her voice sweet but expecting him to refuse.

Johnny looked Matt up and down and then shrugged.

'Might be a better introduction for the film,' Johnny said as Matt was shaking his head.

'I'm very much just in management. All the action is out with the animals,' Matt said and Jemma had to bite her lip to keep her blossoming smile at bay.

'But you do have a natural way with people,' Jemma said, now failing miserably to keep from smiling. Matt seemed to give her the quickest of glares but then sighed.

'Well, Johnny, if you insist.'

Matt and Jemma swapped seats and a make-up artist, whom Jemma hadn't noticed before swept in to give Matt some 'colour'. Jemma had no idea why she hadn't been offered the same service. Maybe they expected keepers to have noses that shone on camera?

'So Matt, maybe you could tell us why the pandas are such a big draw?'

Jemma watched, waiting for Matt to stumble over his words, to not be able to find the right thing to say but as soon as Matt started to speak, Jemma knew the truth. Matt was a natural. It seemed his charm also worked on television, not to mention on the crew themselves.

Jemma shook her head. It wasn't as if she had even wanted to be on TV, but somehow, standing there, watching

Matt make it look so easy she felt a flicker of something. Jealousy, perhaps? She pushed the thought away.

If Matt wanted to be the show's star then good for him and at least it meant she could avoid the cameras and maybe keep her hard-earned reputation intact? She should have been pleased but she felt anything but.

A Star is Born

If Jemma thought that she was going to escape from doing a 'to camera' spot, she was wrong. As soon as they had finished with Matt they appeared in Jemma's section and she had been asked to do an on-camera piece to introduce the park's two panda bears to the TV watching public.

'Our female panda bear is named Lijuan, which means beautiful and graceful,' Jemma said, holding out a hand and pointing to the rotund bear who was chewing on bamboo and then rolled backwards off the rock she was sitting on, before reappearing with a slight look of surprise on her black and white face.

'Our male panda is called Bojing, which means gentle waves. Both pandas come from China. We were one of the first wildlife parks to enter into historic discussions with the Chinese government to arrange for the temporary loan of these endangered creatures.'

Jemma turned her gaze to Bojing who had managed to poke Lijuan in the rear with a bamboo spike. Lijuan for her part seemed unimpressed with what seemed like a rumbled apology from Bojing and used her own bamboo stalk to whack him round the ears.

'They don't seem overly keen on each other,' Johnny Beckett said.

'It is notoriously difficult to breed pandas in captivity,' Jemma said as the bamboo fight continued behind her. Especially when the two bears you had been loaned seemed to have a tetchy relationship, she thought, but decided not to say out loud.

'They don't do very much, do they?' Johnny said as he moved closer to the viewing window. Jemma kept one eye on the cameraman, who now had his camera trained on Johnny, before panning out to get another shot of the pandas, both of whom were doing the panda equivalent of studying their nails.

'What is it you are expecting them to do?' Jemma asked, trying to keep her voice neutral. An image of the five minutes of 'Filthy Rich' appeared in her mind and she told herself firmly that there was no way they were going to set up the pandas to have a full-on physical fight as two of the posh girls had had on screen, no doubt choreographed for the benefit of the viewing public.

'I don't know . . . anything that's a bit more, you know, lively.'

Jemma mouthed the word 'lively'. Clearly Johnny Beckett didn't know much about pandas.

'Pandas in the wild have few predators so as a species they don't need to be able to run or hide,' Jemma started to say.

'So they just sit around all day and ignore each other?'

Jemma sighed. In truth that was pretty much all Bojing and Lijuan did all day — that, and eat their body weight in bamboo.

'No, they spend a fair amount of time eating,' Jemma said but one glance at Johnny's face and she knew she was making it worse. 'They climb trees sometimes.'

Johnny and the rest of the film crew stared at Jemma and then as one looked back at the pandas.

Bojing appeared to have fallen asleep and Lijuan looked like she would soon be doing the same. Jemma could tell from Johnny's expression that he didn't have a clue about pandas' nature and hadn't thought to find out.

'With few natural predators and no need to hunt for food, it is one of the issues with keeping pandas in captivity.' Rosie's voice sounded from beside Jemma and Jemma watched as Rosie's 100-watt smile was clocked by both Johnny and the cameraman, who winked at Rosie.

Rosie smiled and carried on talking.

'Animal enrichment is a key part of our role as caretakers for this amazing but mysterious species.'

Johnny's eyes lit up and he turned his

attention away from the pandas and to Rosie.

'Could you say that again, but to the camera?' he asked eagerly. Rosie smiled again and shrugged as if it didn't matter to her either way.

'As long as Jemma doesn't mind?' Rosie said in a kind of mock conspiratorial way to Johnny, as if Jemma wasn't standing right beside her.

'I don't mind at all,' Jemma said, feeling the need to reply before Johnny relayed the request to her as if they were ten-year-olds in the school playground.

'Rosie is the head keeper for the pandas and will be able to tell you all about their enrichment programme.'

Jemma smiled, but she knew it was dull in comparison to Rosie's. She needn't have bothered since the film crew and Johnny were now getting to shoot their new star. Jemma stood and watched for a few minutes.

Like Matt, Rosie seemed to be a natural and it meant that Jemma was off the hook. Rosie seemed not only comfortable in front of the camera, but Jemma was well aware that Rosie was keen to be there, too, which worked out for everyone. Maybe this wouldn't be such a disaster, after all?

Two hours later and whilst standing in the small break room, eating her lunch on the hoof, and Jemma knew that had been wishful thinking.

'Have you seen what Rosie has been up to?' Melissa, one of the keepers who looked after the great apes, had just walked into the room. 'I can't believe it! It's certainly thinking outside the box . . . ' Melissa's enthusiastic commentary dried up when she realised that Jemma was also in the room.

'Oh, hi, Jemma,' Melissa said, flustered.

'Hi, Melissa, Ted,' Jemma said with a nod of her head. 'Sounds like Rosie has been coming up with some new ideas?'

Ted and Melissa exchanged looks as Ted shrugged, as if to say, 'You opened your mouth, now you'd better tell her.'

Melissa looked slightly panicked and

Jemma felt sorry for her. The last thing she wanted to do was put Melissa on the spot, but she did need to know.

Rosie was a great keeper and passionate about her animals but Jemma couldn't help but wonder what the film crew, and Johnny Beckett in particular, might have encouraged her to do.

'I heard it was something to do with making the enclosure and experience more lifelike for them,' Melissa said, not looking Jemma in the eye.

'Perhaps you should go and see for yourself, lass?' Ted said. He had no trouble looking Jemma in the eye and his message was clear. It was probably a good idea to go quickly.

Jemma wanted to run but knew that she shouldn't. If she started to run, members of the public and not to mention other park staff, would know there was something wrong. And that was the last thing they needed.

Jemma's mind tried to imagine what was going on at the panda enclosure, but nothing she had conjured up came close to what she saw when she got there.

Bojing and Lijuan were sitting in the same spot they had been in earlier. They were both awake now and staring at the spectacle that was playing out in front of their enclosure.

Someone, and Jemma was pretty sure it was Rosie, was dressed up in a panda bear suit. The film crew were recording the event as the person in the panda suit seemed to be attempting to mimic panda behaviour.

Jemma stood stock still as her brain tried to process what was happening.

Only this morning, the wildlife park had been a place of education and important work in preserving species on the brink and now it had been turned into . . . she wasn't even sure what it had been turned it to but it was going to make the park a laughing stock the world over.

'What is going on?' Jemma shouted. She had meant to speak normally, but her emotions had overwhelmed her, and it came out as a yell.

Not that it mattered, since it seemed everyone was ignoring her. Everyone, except the bears who, if Jemma didn't know better, were looking like they were in need of an explanation, too. Jemma forced herself to keep walking and managed to weave her way through the crowd of visitors that had congregated.

'Mr Beckett, what is the meaning of this?' Jemma asked but Johnny Beckett seemed to be too enthralled in the performance in front of him to take much notice.

She could hear muffled conversation from the crowd and from what she could make out it seemed the visitors thought that something very strange was going on.

Jemma had had enough. Everyone was ignoring her and so she walked in front of the camera and grabbed the panda suit by the arm.

'Rosie!' Jemma managed to keep the yell to more of a hiss between gritted teeth this time. 'What on earth are you doing?' she added, trying out a smile on the crowd who just stared back at her, looking collectively bewildered.

Rosie stopped jumping around and making snarling noises and looked at Jemma as if she was the one dressed up like a panda.

'What does it look like I'm doing?'

Jemma was tempted to answer that question but decided that since there were young children present, it was probably best not to, so instead she just raised an eyebrow.

Rosie sighed dramatically.

'Surely it's obvious that I am pretending to be another panda, a female panda.'

Personally Jemma thought it was obvious that Rosie had lost the plot somewhere but kept that to herself.

'Perhaps the more important question is why?' Jemma said, giving Rosie the kind of stares that usually spoke volumes.

'Female pandas in the wild are territorial,' Rosie said the words slowly as if Jemma might have a problem understanding her. 'I thought that it might be more realistic for Lijuan if she had some competition. Might help her to see Bojing in a more positive light.'

Jemma counted to ten under her breath as she let her eyes stray to the pandas, both of whom seemed to have their heads cocked to one side as if they were the ones trying to understand another animal's behaviour.

'I see,' Jemma said, although in truth she really didn't. It wasn't exactly a scientifically approved approach. 'And you chose to do this with the film crew here because . . . ?'

'It was their idea!' Rosie said cheerfully. 'I was explaining about how pandas live in the wild and Johnny suggested that we try to recreate the situation as closely as we can.

'He wanted me to go in with them but I pointed out that under Health and Safety legislation we aren't allowed.' Rosie looked as if she were the kid in class who was expecting to earn a house point for good behaviour.

Jemma shook her head. What had happened to her perfectly sensible head keeper?

'Jemma, darling?' Johnny said loudly and fixed her with his cheesiest grin. 'I don't suppose you could speak to Rosie later about whatever it is that is concerning you? It's just that we are sort of in the middle of something here?'

Jemma opened her mouth to say something but she knew it was no use. The only person who could put a stop to this craziness was Matt Darnell. She was going to march up there to his office and demand that he put a stop to it — now.

* * *

Jemma didn't wait to be shown through. She just walked past Matt's secretary and banged on the door, which was half open anyway.

'Jemma, perfect timing as always,' Matt said as Jemma walked into the room. He was smiling like a child on the first day of the long summer holidays and Jemma wondered if he knew something she didn't.

'Well, I think we can agree it's been a fantastic first day.'

'Fantastic?' Jemma said, trying not to yell, 'Your supposed wildlife documentary crew has proved to be everything I suspected them to be. They aren't interested in the wildlife, at least not unless it is doing something sensational! Do you have any idea what is going on, right now, outside the panda enclosure?'

Matt's eyes had gone wide and he seemed to be making a gesture with his head.

★   ★   ★

Jemma wondered if she had finally got through to him and perhaps they could send Johnny and his crew home, right now. But suddenly Jemma could feel heat on the side of her face and didn't need to turn around to know that a camera crew had magically appeared, and no doubt recorded her outburst.

'Well, it may not have been entirely what we were expecting but I think the rough footage can be put together to make something that will touch the hearts of the public,' Matt said, forcing a smile on to his face which didn't have the usual charm to it.

'I'm sure the public will be fascinated by the lengths that we go to, to ensure that our animals have as close to the wild experience as possible . . . '

Matt appeared to be trying to tell her something, but Jemma had no idea what. Clearly his words were for the benefit of the film crew and no doubt to keep Johnny on his side, should he see this footage. But Jemma didn't care.

The wildlife park's reputation was on the line here, not to mention her own and that was before she considered what it might be doing to her animals.

She shook herself. That last bit was probably unfair, the pandas had looked more bemused than anything else, but still.

The camera was fixed on her face, so Jemma fought to keep her expression neutral and to think of something that she could say to get her message across to Matt without losing her cool.

'Perhaps we could have a planning meeting over dinner?' Matt said and there was a note in his voice that Jemma couldn't place.

'Er . . . ' Jemma started to say as the cameraman swung the camera from Matt back to her for a close-up of her reaction. Jemma couldn't for the life of her work out why this conversation was important to documentary.

'I think perhaps we should have a discussion of some ground rules that we could share with Mr Beckett and his crew? I don't suppose you will have time in your busy day today for a meeting?'

'Sure. Same time as yesterday?' she asked, wanting more than anything to get out of the office

'Sounds good, I'll see you then,' Matt said, looking first at Jemma and then back at the computer on his desk.

'Right,' Jemma said feeling that 'wrong' would have been a better word. Even in her wildest imaginings, she could not have dreamed up today's events.

Cold Encounter

Jemma arrived at the pub first and ordered a white wine spritzer. She thought she deserved a large glass of wine but had decided that she needed to focus.

Matt was not in attendance yet and Jemma wondered if Betty was giving Matt an earful about being out two nights in a row. Her mind's eye conjured up an image of Betty, young, pretty and the type of woman who hung on Matt's every word. Perfect for him, she decided.

Jemma scanned the pub and waved hello to several locals before her eyes settled on the film crew and Johnny, who had commandeered the largest table in the bar and were tucking into large plates of pub food.

Matt arrived just as Jemma was beginning to wonder if it was worth ordering food before the kitchens shut for the day.

'Sorry I'm late.'

Jemma shrugged as if wasn't particularly important as Matt flashed her his most impressive grin, that Jemma knew would have made most women go weak at the knees but not her. She had more important things to focus on and besides, with Betty in the picture, Matt was a no-go area as far as Jemma was concerned.

Matt sat down as Maggie walked over and the same performance as the night before was repeated.

'So, how was your day?' Matt said with a twinkle in his eye.

Jemma stared. How could Matt be joking about the events of the day? Before the day had started she had been worried that it would be embarrassing but now she was worried about the impact it might have on the park's reputation. Jemma didn't need to say anything as Matt seemed to have taken in her expression.

'Look, I know it wasn't the most auspicious start.'

Jemma raised an eyebrow. She wasn't even going to dignify that comment with an answer.

'Look, you may not believe me, but the park is as important to me as it is to you,' Matt said, and his words were earnest but, since Jemma had seen him charm his way before, she was not convinced.

'I suspect for completely different reasons,' Jemma said, and her voice was cold. She hadn't meant it to be and she knew she was probably being unfair. But her sole concern was the welfare of the animals whereas she suspected his was more to do with the park being a profitable venture than anything else.

When Jemma looked up she could see Matt's face was frozen in a look of being deeply insulted and she felt a blush begin to colour her cheeks. She barely knew Matt so it was unfair of her to assume she knew his motives.

'Is that what you think?' he said but his words sounded as if they were being strangled.

Jemma shook her head.

'I'm sorry, that was unfair. It's just we had so many people interested in investing in the park but all they seemed to be concerned with was how much money they could make.'

'And so you automatically think I am one and the same?' Matt said, and the hurt had been replaced by a kind of quiet fury.

'I did and for that I apologise,' Jemma said, feeling guilty and confused all at the same time. She wondered how the evening had deteriorated so quickly and more than that, she felt exhausted from the day, not to mention the worry of the last six months.

Matt nodded but seemed unable to speak. Their dinner arrived, and they ate in silence as Maggie watched them from the bar. Jemma didn't turn around, but she was fairly sure that they had the full attention of the film crew as well. This day really didn't feel like it could get any worse. Matt had eaten all of his dinner before Jemma had managed half of hers.

'I think under the circumstances it would be best if we pick this up at work tomorrow. Nine o'clock in my office?' Matt said, all business-like.

Jemma nodded, as she had a mouthful of chips, and Matt was gone out of the door before she could say anything else. Jemma looked at the remaining half of her dinner and knew that she wouldn't be able to eat it, especially not with the eyes of everyone in the pub on her.

She ducked down and scrabbled in her bag for sufficient money to pay, and left it on the table before scurrying out of the door and heading for the safety of home.

★ ★ ★

Jemma hadn't slept well. All night her mind seemed determined to replay the events of the day with particular focus on the events at the pub.

She couldn't work Matt out. He was

normally so jovial, as if nothing bothered him, but her comments seemed to have really got to him, in a way she had not intended. In the early hours she had come to the conclusion it was because her accusation was true. But then again maybe he genuinely did have an interest in saving wild animals from extinction?

The problem was she just couldn't figure out which it was. And not only that but she had a meeting with him first thing which seemed like it was going to be strained at best.

Standing in front of the mirror, she could see bags under her eyes and a paleness which shouldn't be seen in someone who spent most of her working days outside.

Jemma never felt like serious animal biologists should be concerned with their appearance but today it felt different. She felt like she needed to present a good face to the world, and not just Matt. Before she could talk herself out of it she picked up the powder and blusher and added some much-needed colour to her face.

Jemma was early, and Matt's door was closed. The receptionist had asked her to take a seat and Jemma was trying not to obsess over whether Matt was keeping her waiting to make a point or was simply busy.

She pushed the thought from her mind, telling herself it didn't matter. She needed to work alongside Matt, but it wasn't necessary for them to be friends.

If they could both agree on what was best for the animals then that was fine by Jemma, or so she tried to convince herself as she ignored the burning in her chest.

Betty, she told herself firmly. No point in getting any other ideas, think of Betty!

A shadow fell over Jemma and she looked up. Matt was standing over her, with a curious look on his face.

'Are you OK?' His voice sounded like he was genuinely concerned, and Jemma thought that perhaps things weren't going to be quite as frosty as she had expected.

'I'm fine,' Jemma said, forcing herself to smile up at him. Her heart sank again when it wasn't returned.

Matt merely nodded and gestured for her to follow him. Jemma knew it was unusual for him to be so solemn and the gaze of the receptionist told Jemma that she had never seen Matt like this before, either.

'Would you like tea or coffee, Mr Darnell?' the receptionist asked.

'No, thank you, Tina. This will be a short meeting.'

Jemma followed Matt into his office, feeling as if she had been summoned to the headmaster's office for a telling off. Jemma felt like she ought to say something to clear the air, perhaps apologise again but in the time it took her to decide what to say, Matt had already started to speak.

'Right, thanks for coming in. I know that you're busy.'

Jemma opened her mouth to say it was fine, but Matt looked like he wanted to get on with whatever he had to say and so Jemma closed it again.

'I've had a meeting with Mr Beckett and explained some of your concerns.'

Jemma stared. She knew they hadn't actually got around to talking about her concerns, which meant Matt had assumed he knew what she was worried about.

Even the thought that he would do such a thing was annoying to her. She might have been wrong about his priorities but today he was making it clear that he wasn't interested in what she had to say.

'Whilst he is not exactly happy, he has agreed to abide by the rules.'

'And they would be?' Jemma asked archly. Two could play at this game, she thought.

'I have asked Mr Beckett to refer any decisions with regards to filming the bears to you first. He must have your approval of anything other than background shots.' Matt's voice was cold and it was so unlike him that Jemma had the urge to beg for forgiveness, even though she knew she had already apologised. If he couldn't accept that, then that was up to him.

Jemma swallowed the sudden lump in her throat. This meeting was making her feel like crying. It was so unlike her. She was always business-like and as long as the animals' welfare was priority number one, she never let anything else bother her. She shook her head to try and clear it. She was just tired, that was all.

'Of course,' Jemma said going for business-like but thinking it probably sounded as if she was trying to score a point back. 'If there's nothing else, I'll get back to work.'

It was a statement more than a question and Matt nodded before leaning over to press a button on his phone.

'Tina, can you find me the contact details of our main restaurant suppliers? I want to review their contracts.'

'Of course, Mr Darnell,' Tina said as Jemma made it to the door. Surely that was the worst of it, over and done with. She would get back to focusing on the animals and Matt could focus on balancing the books and raising the profile of the park. Perhaps their paths wouldn't need to cross much in the future.

Jemma knew that thought should have been comforting but somehow it was anything but.

The Food of Love . . . ?

The park had opened minutes before, but few visitors had made it as far as the giant panda enclosure and for that Jemma was grateful. She knew something was going on when she had approached the entrance to the Animal Kingdom.

The park was never quiet, of course. The animals made almost as much noise as the visitors, but this was different. This was music, and not just any music. This was music to fall in love with and it seemed to be coming from the direction of the panda enclosure.

On a table in front of the enclosure was the old beat-up CD player from the staff room. It was blaring a romantic classic. The music was so loud that Jemma could feel her teeth rattle. There was no-one else in sight.

Jemma pressed the off button and even though the music stopped, her ears still rang. The staff gate that led to the food preparation area of the pandas swung open and Rosie appeared, looking cheerful as always.

'Why have you turned the music off?' Rosie asked, turning to gesture at the two pandas who Jemma could have sworn had paws over their ears. 'I think they like it.'

'It's too loud,' Jemma said. 'It's disturbing the other animals, not to mention our visitors.'

'I was thinking last night,' Rosie said, ignoring Jemma's comment, 'maybe we just need to get the pandas in the mood for romance.'

Jemma stared at Rosie, sure she was joking. But there was no tell-tale sign, no twitching of the lips. Jemma knew it wasn't the first of April, so it couldn't be that.

'Rosie . . . ' Jemma said but then realised that she didn't really know what to say.

'Look, we have tried all the conventional methods, all the scientific ones.

Maybe it's the time for out-of-the-box thinking?'

Jemma stared at the pandas. In that respect at least, Rosie wasn't wrong. The breeding season was coming to an end and it appeared that Bojing and Lijuan were at best intolerant of each other, and at worst mortal enemies.

'I think if we can create the right mood, then who knows?' Rosie shrugged. 'Giant pandas aren't so different from humans. Women need to be wooed.'

Jemma looked quickly at Rosie, sure that she must be joking but Rosie's face was deadly serious.

'Wooed?' Jemma asked weakly.

'Yes, you know,' Rosie said before casting a sideways glance at Jemma, that Jemma took to be a sign that she thought it was probably a long time since Jemma had been wooed by anyone. 'Gifts, the right lighting, mood music and dinner.'

'And how do we go about all of that?' Jemma asked, although in truth she didn't really want to know.

'Well, I thought we could start with

the right music. I did wonder about that, though,' Rosie said thoughtfully, and Jemma saw a glimmer of hope that perhaps Rosie was hadn't completely lost the plot.

'Wondered what?' Jemma asked.

'The music we have is all sung in English. I'm not sure it will have the right effect, so I've ordered a CD online which has Cantonese love songs on it.'

Jemma closed her eyes in the hope that when she opened them she would be back in bed, before the day had started.

When she opened her eyes, she realised that Johnny and the motley crew of cameraman and sound technician were back.

Johnny looked as if he were waiting to ask if she were happy for him to film, and that the very fact he had to ask her was at great personal expense. Rosie also turned to her expectantly. Apparently she had been made aware of the rules, too.

'Fine,' Jemma said, 'turn the music

back on but if the bears, or any of the other animals, show any sign of distress, it goes off.'

'Of course,' Rosie said and she now seemed to have joined the group of people Jemma had affronted today. Jemma took a deep breath and tried to smile at Rosie. The last thing she needed was to fall out with her colleague and friend.

'I can't say I'm convinced by your plan but who knows, you might just be leading the world in a new approach,' Jemma said, aiming for conciliation. Rosie looked slightly less ruffled and turned to look from Jemma to the bears.

'Look,' Rosie said, pointing and smiling triumphantly.

Jemma had to admit that the two bears were now marginally closer together and it was just possible that they had briefly made eye contact.

Jemma could feel a vein start to throb in her head and lifted up a hand to massage it and then, catching a glimpse of the cameraman panning the camera towards her, she forced her face into a more neutral expression.

She knew she should look enthused, but it was about as much as she could manage.

Jemma had known that she had her work cut out for her. Saving the park was going to be an ongoing battle but she couldn't understand how Matt had settled on Johnny and his 'documentary' as the answer to all their woes.

Was he too proud to admit he had made a mistake? Was he really ready to risk the park's reputation to save face?

Whatever Jemma's feelings, which seemed to change like the wind direction, she couldn't believe that he would take things that far.

Jemma flicked her eyes to Rosie, who was watching the pandas, completely enraptured, and Jemma was fairly sure that wasn't just because the cameras were focused on her. Was Jemma so resistant to Rosie's plan because it hadn't been her idea?

For a few moments the music died and the pandas, with heads tilted to one side, looked almost relieved, as if it might mean they got some peace and quiet at last.

Perhaps Jemma could persuade them that if they could just get their act together, so to speak, she could get rid of the film crew?

Jemma shook her head. Now she was treating wild animals like people. Perhaps the lunacy was catching.

Outrageous Accusation

There was something, Jemma decided, about listening to love songs in another language. You didn't need to understand the language to know that the songs were tales of lost love in tragic circumstances.

The pandas didn't look happy. But then they were being subjected to Chinese love songs for 12 hours a day. Rosie had wanted to leave the music on 24 hours but Jemma had put her foot down. Bojing and Lijuan, in her opinion, were suffering enough.

There was no doubt that they now seemed to be sitting closer together but Jemma was sure it was a shared experience of misery rather than any romantic feelings.

Her own romantic feelings were troubling her too and they weren't making her any happier than the pandas.

If anyone asked why she was looking so tired she simply pointed out that she had to deal with the film crew and their demands on a daily basis, not to mention all the other issues that the large mammal section was currently dealing with and that was keeping her awake at night.

She would never admit the real reason. The truth of the matter was something that she was definitely keeping to herself.

Every night when she closed her eyes, all she could think about was Matt. Her mind seemed to be caught in some kind of time loop and replayed the fateful conversation at the pub and then every coldly professional meeting they had had since.

What was most puzzling was why it was bothering her so much. If anything, she would have said it was the best possible outcome.

Matt was clearly in a relationship with Betty and Jemma's only serious romantic relationship had ended when she discovered her boyfriend, George, was seeing one of her friends behind her back.

That day she had vowed she would never be the other woman, however she felt about the man in question. She would never cause that kind of pain to anyone else.

But there was something about Matt that was getting under her skin. She shook her head to try to shift the image of him looking hurt at her suggesting he was more interested in money than the animals' welfare.

That was a low blow and she was embarrassed now that she had ever said it, but she also knew that it was more than that. It wasn't just guilt she was feeling at upsetting him. Seeing the pain in his face had caused her pain too, as if he was the last person in the world that she would ever want to hurt and that she couldn't understand.

It wasn't as if she spent her life trying to hurt people, in fact the opposite was true. Having been hurt herself she did her best to get on with everyone she came across and surely her new boss should be no exception. But why did she feel so bad about Matt?

After George, she had thrown herself into her work and it had been enough. She had such a passion for animal welfare and the survival of species at risk that it felt only appropriate that she throw herself into her mission whole-heartedly.

She had no time for romance and had managed to avoid it since George, and wasn't sorry that she didn't have that added complication in her life.

So why was her heart betraying her now? It wasn't as if anything could come of her and Matt — she wouldn't let it.

Jemma forced her attention back to the bears who were disconsolately chewing on the fresh bamboo that Jemma had placed in their outside area before letting them out of their sleeping quarters.

What she needed was to focus on

work and forget about Matt, that was the answer. She had managed it before, when George had broken her heart, and she could do it again. Besides all that, Matt clearly wasn't interested in her, so it would all work out. She just needed to stay focused.

'Morning,' a voice said in her ear. Jemma jumped and let out a squeal, with one hand over her heart and the other reaching out for the railings that stopped visitors from getting too close to the panda enclosure.

She knew whose the voice was instantly, she just couldn't work out if it was her mind playing a cruel trick or if Matt had actually just appeared beside her.

A quick glance to one side told her it was Matt and he looked concerned.

'Sorry, did I startle you?'

'No, no. I was just . . . '

'Lost in thought?' Matt said, and his charming smile was firmly in place.

Jemma took a deep breath to give herself time to put on a composed expression. Matt could not read her mind. He had no idea what she had been thinking about.

'Trying to work out if the music is helping,' Jemma said, trying to hide her flushed face at the lie she was telling.

'Well, they seemed to be sitting closer than they were.' Matt was now peering into the enclosure and wincing slightly as a particularly high-pitched soprano took over the latest tragic love song. Even the film crew, set up outside the enclosure, were wearing what appeared to be earplugs.

'I think that's just shared misery rather than anything else,' Jemma said, wondering how Matt might respond but knowing it was the truth.

'Maybe they will mate just to make the music stop,' Matt said softly so that only Jemma could hear.

A multi generational family had appeared to stare at the pandas and the youngest child had both hands covering his ears to block out the music.

Jemma could feel a smile twitch at

her lips and had to fight to hold it back. If she smiled now, it could be interpreted as flirting and that was the last thing either of them needed. Think of Betty, she told herself firmly. Think how George made you feel.

'You might be right, although I'm not sure that's really what we want to go for in a wildlife park that's aim is to give them a life experience as close to the wild as possible.'

'Maybe this is what happens in mainland China? It could explain why the species struggles to breed.'

Jemma looked up sharply, momentarily concerned that Matt was being serious, but he was wearing a sort of half grin as if he wasn't sure his humour was going to go down very well.

'Might explain why they chose to live far up in the mountains away from humans,' Jemma said. It really felt like Matt was offering an olive branch and Jemma couldn't resist it.

Maybe if they cleared the air she would be able to sleep and focus on her work? Perhaps if they were back on friendly terms her heart would be quiet too. Jemma risked a glance in Matt's direction and saw what she was sure was relief on his face. Perhaps he had felt it too? That sense that something was off, and it had unsettled him as well.

'Any issues with our film crew friends that I should know about?' Matt asked, his voice returning to his normal concern, business-like but friendly.

'Other than a discussion about not banging on the glass, no. I think we're managing to keep them in check.'

Jemma was watching Johnny as Rosie started to read something from a piece of paper in front of her. It sounded like Chinese. Not that Jemma was an expert any more than Rosie was. It looked like it must be some kind of dramatic, romantic poetry judging by the way Rosie was acting as she said the words. One glance at the pandas told her that they were as nonplussed by the whole thing as she was.

The film crew however seemed

entranced and Johnny was rubbing his hands together, clearly happy with his latest bit of filming. Jemma could feel Matt studying her and so kept her eyes fixed on the pandas.

She wasn't sure whether it was because she didn't want to see something that might give her heart hope, or if she didn't want to give him any encouragement. Her mind conjured up Betty once more and that was enough to keep her strong.

'Well, thank you for all your hard work,' Matt said, 'it is appreciated. Let me know if you need any assistance.'

Jemma did look up now. To do otherwise would seem childish. She thought she saw a flash of something in Matt's face but whatever it was, was quickly replaced by a professional work sort of expression, not stony like before, but definitely not overly friendly.

'I will, thank you. I'd best be getting on,' Jemma added when it seemed like they were going to be stuck in the awkwardness.

'And I have a meeting,' Matt said, smiling tightly and then he strode off in the direction of the park management suite. Jemma watched him go. She was relieved that they had cleared the air, but she had the distinct feeling that even that wasn't going to be enough to shake the feeling that her heart wanted more.

'I knew it!' a voice said in Jemma's ear and she jumped, not just because the voice seemed to have appeared from nowhere but because it had a south London accent that she recognised as belonging to Johnny Beckett.

'Mr Beckett!' Jemma gasped, one hand on her chest as she realised the man was standing six inches away from her and wondering if she was going to have to have an embarrassing conversation with him about the need to respect her personal space.

'You fancy him,' he said, pointing a finger at her nose.

Jemma took a giant step backwards.

'What on earth do you mean?' The

question was out of her mouth before she could consider the fact that she didn't need to get into this sort of conversation with him. Her personal life was none of his business.

'There's no point hiding, love. We can all see it.' Johnny threw his arms wide and the cameraman and sound woman all nodded. Jemma blinked as she realised that she was once again on camera.

'Well, thank you for your input,' Jemma said, walking out through the keeper door, which Matt had left open, and into the public area, which was now full of families.

As soon as she was out there she knew it was a mistake. The presence of the public wouldn't stop Johnny Beckett, like it might any other decent person.

'You can't hide it from us, Jemma, not to mention the fact the viewers will love it. It will add a real twist to the documentary. You know — liven things up a bit.'

Jemma turned on the spot, mouth

open, ready to point out that they were here to film the wildlife, not her, but there was no way she was going to discuss anything like that with Johnny whilst the camera was rolling.

'You keep fighting it, darling. Makes for better viewing!' Johnny said, before turning to check the camera was following Jemma's every move.

'My personal life has nothing to do with the film, or the pandas. They are why you're here and so I suggest you keep your focus firmly on them,' Jemma said.

Johnny crossed his arms and looked at her knowingly.

'Maybe it's your fault?' he said, raising a challenging eyebrow.

Jemma knew she should walk away and ignore him but she couldn't.

'What is that supposed to mean?'

'It means, darling, that maybe your panda bears are modelling you and young Matthew. Star-crossed lovers but never destined to share their true feelings?'

Jemma could feel fury rising up inside her. She glared at Johnny, then remembered the camera and turned on her heel and walked in the direction of the keepers' station beside the panda enclosure.

Once the door was closed behind her, she closed her eyes and leaned against the wall. She couldn't bear to imagine what Matt's reaction to Beckett's ideas would be. Surely he would think the TV man was losing the plot? But what if he took it seriously?

There was a bark from the enclosure and Jemma watched as Lijuan clubbed Bojing around the head. Bojing grumbled and walked off to the other side of the enclosure, to his side.

Jemma sighed. She had no idea how she was going to get the two pandas together, let alone keep her hard earned professional reputation intact. Not when Johnny Beckett and his film crew had decided that her love life was the most interesting thing about the park.

Breakdown in Communications

Jemma heard the radio crackle at her hip. Whoever was using the radio was clearly a novice. There was a crackle of static and the dead air followed by what sounded like a person clearing their throat.

'Er . . . hello? Jemma? Is this thing working?'

Despite the crackle Jemma knew whose voice it was, she just couldn't work out why he was using the radio.

'Jemma here,' Jemma replied in her most professional voice. Someone had to maintain the decorum, after all. Her radio beeped, and she didn't need the red light to flash to tell her that Matt still had his 'send' button depressed which meant that she wouldn't be able to reply. She sighed and started to make her way to the management offices in the centre of the park.

'Why is this thing so difficult to use? Do we need to replace them? We can't have equipment that doesn't work!' Matt was starting to sound frustrated. 'Can anyone even hear me? I need to talk to Jemma about the filming and I haven't got time to go out and find her — wherever she is.'

Jemma quickened her pace. She felt a sudden desire to run, hoping against hope that Matt would realise that his every word was being transmitted all around the park and that literally hundreds of people would be listening. Please don't mention Johnny Beckett's plan, she said silently and repeated it like a mantra.

'It's the perfect hook for the documentary — two pandas trying to find love and two people. It's almost too perfect! Your relationship with Jemma reads perfectly on screen.' Johnny's voice filtered over the airwaves.

Jemma tried to keep her face

professional, as if the words had no impact but she drew the stares of Kevin and Dana, who worked within the entomology department, as she hurried past. They said nothing, but Jemma could feel her cheeks colour as she heard muffled laughter when they clearly thought she was out of earshot.

That was it. She had had it with Beckett and his film crew. Whatever happened they were going to leave the park and go home. The park had signed up for a wildlife documentary — not some fly-on-the-wall, invasive, trashy reality show. And when she saw Matt she was going to give him an ultimatum.

Her radio crackled again, and she was half tempted to turn the volume down completely to save herself the embarrassment, but she couldn't quite bring herself to do it. It was like watching something terrible happen in front of you and not being able to drag your eyes away.

If Johnny was going to share his thoughts on how her supposed feelings for Matt could liven up the documentary then she wanted to know exactly what he said. The more she knew, the better her argument to cancel the agreement and get rid of the film crew once and for all.

'It's TV gold! Matt, surely you can see that. It will be a hit for sure and that can only be good for the zoo.'

Jemma groaned. As she walked up past the entrance to the gift shop she could see the eyes of the staff following her every step. They all had access to the radio, too, in case of an emergency, and it was clear that they had heard every word.

Lifting her head high and putting her shoulders back, she walked past as if nothing untoward had happened. Surely that was the best thing to do when a lunatic film maker shared his thoughts with the whole park.

What she couldn't figure out was how he had discovered how she felt. She had worked so hard to keep the ridiculous feelings secret; and they were ridiculous, no doubt the result of too much stress and not enough sleep, thanks in no part to having a camera follow her every move.

She pulled the door to the management offices open with more force than she intended, and the glass door banged loudly against the wall.

All eyes in the office looked up sharply and Jemma didn't need to ask them if they had heard Johnny's pronouncement. A few stared openly and the rest looked away as if they were embarrassed for her. Jemma wasn't sure which reaction was worse.

Tina stood up and gave what Jemma interpreted as a supportive smile.

'Jemma, Mr Darnell has been trying to raise you on the radio.' Tina flushed, as Jemma's expression told her that she was well aware of that fact. 'If you come with me, I'm sure he will be free to see you now.'

Tina carried the look of someone who had unintentionally made a difficult situation worse. She scurried off, her heels clicking on the laminate floor, in the direction of Matt's office.

The door was closed, and so Tina knocked but opened the door straight away, not waiting to be asked to come in.

'Mr Darnell, I have Jemma here for you,' Tina said, stepping aside so that Jemma could make her way into the room. 'I thought you would want her brought straight through.'

Tina didn't wait for a reply, simply scurried out of the door and closed it behind her. Clearly, she did not want to be around for whatever was going to happen next. Matt was sitting behind his desk and the offending radio was on the desk.

Johnny was standing by the window taking in the view of the park that the offices provided and acting as if he were an Oscar-winning documentary maker, preparing for his next shot.

'Ah, Jemma, I've been trying to raise you on the radio, but it doesn't seem to be working.'

Jemma eyed him carefully to see if he

was trying to cover up his grave error or if in fact he was completely unaware that everything he said had been transmitted around the park.

His face appeared open and relaxed, so Jemma decided that either he was a good liar, or he genuinely had no idea.

'The radio is working fine. I heard every word,' Jemma said, unable to keep the iciness from her tone.

'It's all a bit new to me, I'm afraid, but thank you for taking time out of your busy schedule to come and speak with me.' Matt sounded a little unsure, as if he knew that he had done something wrong but had no idea what.

'I heard every word, as did everyone else in the park.' Jemma spat the words out through clenched teeth and couldn't resist the urge to glare in Johnny's direction.

'Ah, I see,' Matt said, shifting uncomfortably in his seat. 'Well, that was unfortunate . . . '

Jemma cut him off with a wave of her hand.

'All of my colleagues, not to mention my team, heard him,' Jemma pointed at Johnny's back, who appeared completely unfazed by any accusations and continued to enjoy the view, 'speaking about my private life and making spurious accusations.'

Matt pursed his lips together in an effort to suppress the smile that was tugging at his lips. Jemma turned her glare on him and it had the opposite effect to the one she was going for. He burst out laughing. This at least seemed to grab Johnny's attention.

'I'm sorry, Jemma, but you can't be embarrassed about this. Everyone will know that it's crazy talk. I mean no-one can think that there is some sort of unrequited love between the two of us.'

Jemma knew that she should be glad that he was seeing the funny side, glad that he wasn't even considering that there could be any truth in Johnny's words, but it hurt all the same.

She swallowed and stared at the carpet, digging her fingernails into the palms of her hands as she could feel tears prick at her eyes. She was not going to cry.

'Look, I can see you are angry about this,' Matt said, holding both hands out. Jemma forced herself to look up. She didn't want to give him any reason to think that he was wrong in his interpretation of her reaction.

And of course she was angry! It was better for him to think that than anything else.

'I have a professional reputation to maintain and this outburst is not going to do that any favours — not to mention the fact that this supposedly serious documentary is turning into the worse kind of reality TV.' She managed to say the words out loud.

Matt was right, she was cross about that, but she would never admit that hurt was the overriding emotion for her right now.

'I understand, really I do,' Matt added as he seemed to take in Jemma's expression. 'Your reputation and the reputation of the wildlife park is important to me, too.'

Jemma knew there was a 'but' coming, there was always a 'but'.

'But imagine the coverage this show could bring us. Think of the rise in funding it might bring with it. We could develop better enclosures, ones that are more like the wild and who knows — that might be enough to get our pandas breeding.'

Matt's eyes were glittering at the prospect and Jemma knew that she shared his excitement. It would be amazing. If they could establish a breeding pair then it was possible that China would allow them to keep the bears long term and maybe they could establish their own British-born panda family.

There was also something about sharing that excitement with someone else who felt the same, but Jemma quickly pushed the feelings down. She needed to focus, and those sorts of thoughts did not help.

Money was important, of course it

was, she was sensible enough to know that, but that didn't mean they all had to make fools of themselves on national television.

'I agree it would be a positive for the park to increase its revenue and whilst there are no guarantees that more money would result in a panda cub, it would certainly benefit the animals,' Jemma said.

She saw some of the excitement slip from Matt's features, but she ploughed on regardless. She needed to say what she thought about Johnny's plans for the supposed documentary, to point out the ridiculousness of it all or else be drawn into another crackpot, media-grabbing approach.

Matt's expression nearly made her pause. He looked as if he was rapidly moving back to 'professional and aloof' Matt but there was nothing that Jemma could do about that. She needed to tell him exactly what she thought, whatever the consequences.

What About Betty?

'I was given to understand that the welfare of the animals was your number one priority.' Matt said the words so frostily that Jemma felt like she needed to pull on her winter coat.

Matt had moved back to that place where he was professional and nothing more. Jemma's emotions seemed to somersault once more, and she could only conclude that she would never be happy. Part of her wanted to keep everything professional, but another part of her wanted something more. Something she knew she couldn't have.

'You know it is,' Jemma said, sounding childlike, even to her own ears. She took a deep breath and tried again. 'Creating the best environment for them is my life's work. I just don't think that we should have to sell our souls, not to mention our reputation, to do so.'

There, she had managed to be diplomatic. She had held back all the thoughts that it was Matt's fault that the film crew were here. It was Matt's fault that she had been so embarrassed in front of all her colleagues and it was Matt's fault that she could no longer control her emotions. That last bit was unfair, she knew, but she figured as long as she kept that thought to herself, it could do no harm.

'I'm not sure that you appreciate the financial implications of what you are suggesting.' Matt's emphasis on the 'appreciate' were not lost on Jemma. He was saying that all she had to worry about were the animals, whereas he was responsible for making sure there was sufficient money for the park to stay open.

'I do appreciate that a park such as this must bring in income, really I do.' Jemma had more to say but Matt cut her off with a wave of his hand.

'Then I think we can agree that any income we can generate can only benefit the animals in our care.'

Jemma opened her mouth but found she didn't know what to say. He was right, of course, that without income the park would have to close and she couldn't begin to imagine how difficult it would be to find homes for all their animals, not to mention jobs for their employees.

But were they really that desperate? Desperate enough to plaster their personal lives, whether it was real or designed for a dramatic purpose, on the nation's TV screens.

Matt leaned back in his chair and steepled his fingers. It was a classic management move and so Jemma met his gaze coolly. She wasn't going to back down over this. It was too important.

'The management group has invested a lot of money in the park. Money that you felt was urgently needed to improve habitats. It would be foolish, not to mention fiscally unsound, to reject the opportunity to recoup some of that money so that it can be reinvested in improving the lives of the animals and the experience of the visitors.'

Jemma wanted to ask how much money had been spent on refurbishing the management suite but kept her mouth closed as she battled the two opposing sides that seemed to have formed in her mind.

'Have you even listened to Johnny's idea?' Matt asked, one eyebrow raised.

Jemma wanted to shout out that she didn't need to. Whatever it was, it was no doubt ridiculous in the extreme, not to mention personally and profession-ally embarrassing.

'No, I haven't,' Jemma managed to say, fighting to keep her voice even.

'Well, might I suggest that you take a seat and at least hear Johnny out?'

When he put it like that it sounded so reasonable — that was if you had never watched 'Filthy Rich'.

With a sigh, Jemma took the seat that Matt had indicated. It was clear that she wasn't going to be able to get out of the office and back to work unless she did. She would listen and then repeat her arguments.

There was nothing in her contract to say that she had to partake in a TV documentary. Perhaps Rosie and Matt could pretend to have a relationship? They seemed to enjoy being on camera, after all.

'Johnny? Would you mind repeating your plan?' Matt urged.

'Sure, if Jemma's is ready to hear me out,' Johnny said, throwing himself down in the free chair and swinging one leg over its arm. Matt looked at Jemma expectantly and there was a challenge in his expression. Jemma sighed.

'Yes, of course, please proceed,' Jemma said in her most professional voice and arranged her face into what she hoped conveyed professional courtesy if not actual interest.

'Pandas are cute and all and, in a different age, some boring footage of them chewing on bamboo would probably have been enough.'

Jemma briefly closed her eyes and

forced herself to count to ten. How could Matt even think about letting this guy shoot a film in their park?

'But these days the kids want more. With the internet, they are able to get up close and personal with today's stars and if you want to get them interested in saving the world, you have to pull them in.'

Matt was nodding and Jemma almost laughed at the sight of him taking Johnny so seriously, but then remembered what was at stake so started practising her argument for why they shouldn't allow filming.

'Your relationship makes a nice juxtaposition to that of the bears. If the viewer gets engrossed in that then they'll start to care about the pandas, too.'

Jemma sighed. She couldn't help it. Surely Matt was not buying any of this. He held up his hand and Johnny looked at him expectantly.

'There's only one problem with your plan,' Matt said and Jemma felt a huge wave of relief. If they could agree on this at least, then she could see a time when they might be able to rediscover some form of friendship.

'What if there is no relationship between Jemma and me?'

Jemma's heart sank with the words. She knew she should have been pleased. It was, after all, what she wanted.

Matt was clearly devoted to Betty and Jemma had no doubt misread all the signs and perhaps this was his way of telling her, but it still hurt. Deep down, Jemma still knew that she had feelings for Matt, however much she tried to ignore the fact.

'Doesn't matter,' Johnny said with a shrug. 'Not many of the relationships on these types of shows are. I'll let you into a little secret,' Johnny said, leaning forward. 'A lot of the shows have a script and some of it is entirely made up.'

Matt nodded slowly and then glanced at Jemma who did her best to push down all the conflicting emotions so that nothing would show on her face.

'I can't force you to do this, Jemma. I know that it's not in your contract. And I would never normally ask you to do something like this but the money the film will bring in will be vital to the survival of the park.'

Jemma made herself look Matt in the eye. If she believed him then she also had to believe that he was telling the truth about the financial situation the park found itself in. She had always promised herself she would do whatever it took to make sure her animals had the best, but could she do this?

Being on TV was not something that she had ever aspired to and certainly not in this kind of show but she also knew that wasn't the real problem.

The real problem was whether she could keep her feelings for Matt hidden. She made herself think of Betty and wondered how Matt would explain this all to her.

'What about Betty?' Jemma asked, before she could chicken out.

Matt smiled.

'I'll talk to her and I'm sure she'll understand,' he said. 'She knows how important the park is.'

Jemma nodded. If Matt could do this, then surely she could, too? She let her mind conjure up the wish list that she had secretly written for each group of animals. Matt looked both surprised and relieved.

'But I should make one thing clear, I'm no actress,' Jemma pointed out.

'No need to be,' Johnny said with an expansive grin. 'Just be yourself,' he added with a wink; and that, Jemma thought, was the problem.

Too Close for Comfort

The morning seemed to speed by. Not that Jemma wasn't usually kept busy, but it felt like she was being dragged unwillingly towards lunchtime. Lunchtime, when she had instructions to meet Johnny and the rest of the film crew at the panda enclosure.

She had been working on the staff roster for the following month and dealing with various other admin tasks. Jemma would never admit it out loud, but she felt the need to stay out of the public view, and avoiding her colleagues wasn't such a bad thing either.

She worked with one eye on the clock. Being late was not an option since she didn't want to be summoned over the radio, and so at five minutes to 12 she stood up from her desk and made her way to the panda enclosure.

The park seemed unusually busy for

a week day, or perhaps all of the visitors had decided to visit the pandas all at the same time. Jemma couldn't see over the crowds that had gathered.

'Here she is! Let her through,' Johnny's voice called out over the crowd which parted in a way that Jemma had never been able to manage before.

Walking through the now divided crowd, Jemma could see that directly in front of the panda enclosure was a round table, covered with a table cloth and laid up for what appeared to be silver service. On both sides of the table, two cameras were set up, presumably to be able to track every move of the two diners.

A man in a tuxedo appeared and ushered Jemma to her seat. As Jemma sat down the camera panned in for a close up and Johnny appeared.

'So, Jemma, you find yourself invited to a surprise lunch. Any thoughts?' Johnny said.

Jemma wished she had known what the plan was so that she could have prepared. No-one had said anything about lunch and certainly not the spectacle of a romantic dinner for two, which seemed to have drawn in the crowds.

'Well, it's a little unexpected,' she managed to squeak as she shifted away from the camera which had homed in for a close-up of her face.

'Do you have any clue who your secret admirer might be?' Johnny grinned out at the crowd but all Jemma could do was stare and hope that Matt had spoken to Betty about the plan.

'Jemma!' Matt announced loudly. 'You look lovely!'

Jemma risked a brief glare in his direction. She was wearing her new uniform complete with furry baseball cap and could hardly be described as lovely.

Matt handed her a bunch of flowers and leaned in to kiss her on the cheek. Jemma's reaction was lost due to the sudden cheer and spontaneous clapping that was coming from the crowd.

'Er, thanks,' Jemma said softly, hoping that no-one else could hear her.

'You're welcome,' Matt said with a beam, as if they weren't stuck in an extremely awkward situation being watched by a crowd.

'I thought Bojing might need a few lessons in the art of romance and what lady can resist flowers?' Matt grinned, and Jemma tried to smile back.

'The problem is, I don't know any florists that will deliver to the panda enclosure and besides, Bojing doesn't have any money,' Jemma said, feeling like she ought to at least try to enter into the spirit of things.

She was rewarded by a smattering of laughter from the crowd and Matt's broadening grin.

'I expect the park could sub him,' Matt said and even Jemma had to smile this time. There was still a part of her that couldn't believe her life had become so surreal but at the same time she had to admit that she was starting to relax and see the funny side of things.

If nothing else, the spectacle might draw more people to visit the park and that could only be good for everyone involved. She had dedicated her life to preventing species from going extinct, so surely she could cope with a little embarrassment in order to raise the park's profile.

A figure appeared at the table, dressed in a long black skirt, white shirt and a long white apron. It took Jemma a second to realise that it was Rosie. She held a plate in each hand and smiled coyly at the camera as she placed both dishes in front of the respective diners.

'For your starter today we have prawn cocktail.' Rosie winked at the camera and then sashayed away.

'Well, I suppose it's a classic,' Matt said, looking somewhat doubtfully at his plate. Jemma gingerly skewered a prawn which seemed to be coated in a neon pink sauce.

She was just eating her first mouthful when a man appeared. He was wearing a sombrero and a black waistcoat and was carrying a guitar. Jemma groaned, she couldn't help it, and Matt turned around in his seat just as the man started to strum out his first tune.

Whilst Jemma didn't speak Spanish and so couldn't make out the words, the emotion in the man's voice told her that it was a love song, most likely a tragic one.

The crowd fell silent as if no-one wanted to interrupt the man until the song had reached its conclusion. When the man finished, wiping a tear from his eye, the crowd applauded once more.

Jemma was staring at the pandas who were sitting side by side on one of the rocks in the enclosure. She blinked once and then twice, sure she was dreaming. She didn't think she had ever seen them being voluntarily so close together. Matt had followed her gaze.

'Well, would you look at that? Who would have thought that the answer to their relationship woes was the entertainer from the Mexican restaurant in town?' Matt sounded faintly in awe and Jemma felt a flush of irritation.

'I'm sure it's a coincidence or maybe

they're trying to work out what's happening,' Jemma said. She couldn't believe that the secret to bringing the pandas together was around her and Matt pretending to be in some kind or relationship.

At this point the tuxedo-wearing waiter reappeared and took a deep bow, simultaneously balancing two dishes of food in one hand. The crowd applauded him as he placed the dishes in front of Matt and Jemma.

'Your main course,' the waiter announced. 'Johnny said you should hold hands. The crowd are lapping it up,' he whispered quietly so that only Jemma and Matt could hear.

Matt and Jemma exchanged glances, their hands staying firmly separate.

'He said that you agreed to take direction,' the waiter added.

Jemma didn't remember agreeing to any such thing and had an overwhelming desire to get up and run away. It wasn't just the embarrassment of being watched by a crowd of people, it was more that she didn't know how she would feel if she held Matt's hand.

It was one thing to dream about a person, it was another thing when that dream started to become pseudo reality for the purpose of a TV show.

Jemma didn't have to decide what her move was going to be as Matt made a grab for her hand. It seemed churlish to pull her hand away and so they awkwardly ate their lunch of steak and mashed potatoes using only their forks.

'Ahh,' someone in the crowd murmured. Jemma had to fight to avoid rolling her eyes. Did they really believe what they were seeing was real? But then she followed their collective gazes and saw Bojing retake his seat near to Lijuan.

'Maybe all the bears needed was to see a couple together. You know, being romantic, like,' an older woman said in a loud voice with a thick Yorkshire accent.

Jemma tried to ignore the comment and concentrate on her food, but her eyes were being drawn to the panda enclosure.

It was true — the bears certainly appeared happier in each other's company than they had been. But she was also sure it had nothing to do with the display that was being put on.

Matt squeezed her hand and Jemma felt a flash of heat. Having lunch with Matt might be manageable, but having him so close physically, holding her hand, in what her brain was telling her was a clear sign of affection, was only making things a thousand times worse.

Conflicting Emotions

Dessert was served — Black Forest gateau. Jemma had no idea where Johnny got his menu ideas from, but it seemed likely that it involved an early 1980s recipe book. It brought back memories for Jemma, particularly when she got to the centre of her slice and it was still semi-frozen.

'I haven't had that for years,' Matt said, pushing away his dish and making a show of rubbing his tummy. The crowd giggled. Jemma smiled as that seemed the thing to do. Matt's eyes were on her face and it was as if he couldn't look away.

'Look, Mummy, look!' A small child's voice broke the spell and both Jemma and Matt looked in the direction of the pandas. Bojing was grooming Lijuan's fur and more importantly, Lijuan was letting him.

'Would you look at that?' Matt said softly, his voice filled with awe.

Jemma pushed back her chair and with some reluctance, gently pulled her hand free from Matt's. She walked over to the wall that separated the public from the pandas and watched as Lijuan turned to snuffle Bojing's paw.

She couldn't believe what she was seeing. Finally, the two bears seemed to be able to tolerate the presence of the other. No, more than that, they appeared to be bonding. Unbidden, Jemma could feel tears start to form in her eyes as Matt moved to stand beside her.

'Is that natural behaviour?' he asked. Even the crowd seemed to understand the importance of not disturbing the bears and kept their excitement to low whispers.

Jemma nodded. She didn't think she would be able to speak, at least not without her voice breaking.

'Amazing,' Matt said, and he sounded so genuinely thrilled that it made Jemma's happiness surge and she knew she had no chance of stopping the tears from flowing down her cheeks. When Matt reached down for her hand and gave it a squeeze, Jemma didn't draw back.

To witness the bears' behaviour change was such a moment for her, personally and professionally, that she was only too happy to be able to share it with someone who seemed to understand.

'Get a close-up.' Johnny's voice went some way to break the spell. Jemma knew that the camera was panning in, not on the bears but on the fact that Jemma and Matt were holding hands. Jemma pulled her hand away quickly, but if Matt minded he didn't show it.

Jemma fought the conflicting emotions of hope, and the wrongness of having feelings for a man who was already in a relationship. She was unable to form a sensible reply to the question.

'Jemma and her team work very hard to create the most natural environment they can for the bears,' Matt was saying, 'and I'm sure that has been a key factor in the progress the bears have made.

'With so few surviving in the wild and the difficultly of breeding in captivity, I think we can all agree that this is an important moment for the species and the wildlife park.'

He turned to Jemma and seemed to be under the impression that she would share his smile. She tried, she really did, but something about his reaction told her that she had failed miserably. She was too caught up in trying to settle down her heart that she couldn't focus.

What he thought her lack of smile meant, she could only guess. Did he think that she still thought he was only interested in the park making money? She needed to say something, to salvage the situation but she couldn't think of any words.

'Successful breeding of pandas outside of China has long been fraught with difficulty, but it is an important step in ensuring the future of these magnificent creatures and ensuring they are very real to the next generation who will take forward the responsibility for the survival of this species and all the others that we have here in the wildlife park,' he added.

Matt must have read her detailed report on the current situation that all the large mammals were in worldwide. She had highlighted those that were critically endangered and the issues they faced, as well as giving a detailed report on the breeding programmes that the park was part of.

She stared at Matt. Not only had he read it, but he seemed to have learned the information. She knew now that she had misjudged him. He wasn't just about profit margins. He seemed to care, like she did.

'If you'll excuse me,' he said to the camera with a smile, 'I have work to be getting on with and I think my role here is done. Managing the administration of the park may not be glamorous or exciting but it's still important.' With a curt nod to Jemma, he was gone.

All Jemma could do was watch him go as she tried to work out what had just happened. She could sense that the camera was still focusing on her and in her imagination she suspected that it could also pick up the figure of Matt as he walked away. Perhaps Johnny had been right. All they needed to do was act natural, since they seemed to have created their own drama.

'So Jemma, how do you feel about the romantic gesture of Matt, your boss?' Jemma swallowed the lump that had appeared in her throat and said nothing. 'And how do you feel about its sudden ending?'

Jemma knew exactly how she felt but she wasn't about to share that with anyone, let alone Johnny Beckett and the viewing public. In her head Jemma kept repeating the name 'Betty' over and over to remind herself that Matt was unavailable, even if he did have feelings for her, which she was pretty sure he didn't.

'The lunch was very pleasant but now I need to get back to work. Perhaps you would like to follow me as

I get on with caring for the pandas?' She wanted to add 'because that's what this idiotic reality show is supposed to be about' but she kept the words to herself.

She started to walk away but the crew stayed where they were, clearly waiting for instructions from Johnny, who was looking at Jemma thoughtfully. It might be the stress of recent events but Jemma had the distinct impression that he was conjuring up a new plan and she didn't think she could handle that right now.

'I need to go and clean out the bears' sleeping quarters. You're welcome to come and film me whilst I undertake this important aspect of the care we provide.'

Jemma had one hand in her pocket with her fingers crossed, hoping that they wouldn't find anything interesting in that activity.

In fact, she thought that Rosie had probably already finished the cleaning out, but it was the only place that

Jemma could think of that would take her out of public view.

'I think we'll take some background shots of the visitors,' Johnny said, clearly not keen on getting up close and within smelling distance of clearing up after large mammals.

'That's fine,' Jemma said, trying to keep the relief from her face. She nodded at the cameraman who was turning away from her and she tried to smile at the crowd, but they had lost interest in her now, more focused on getting their faces on TV, if only for a few seconds.

Jemma seized her opportunity and dashed towards the locked gate that would hide her from the world.

With the gate closed behind her and locked — the public weren't allowed in this part of the enclosure and the TV crew had to be accompanied by a member of staff — Jemma finally felt like she had escaped.

'Wasn't that romantic!' Rosie said, clapping her hands and jumping up and down. 'I knew you had a bit of a thing for Matt.' She leaned in towards Jemma conspiratorially. 'I have to admit I'm a bit jealous, but then I met Brett, so all is forgiven.'

'Brett?' Jemma asked hoping to shift the topic from her and Matt, not that there was a 'her and Matt'.

'Cameraman. Gorgeous. Don't tell me you're so smitten with Matt that you hadn't noticed.' Rosie had her hands on her hips now and she looked outraged.

'Right, cameraman,' Jemma said weakly although she was fairly sure she would not be able to pick the gorgeous Brett out in a crowd.

'Understandable, I suppose,' Rosie said, peering at Jemma, 'especially now that it seems Matt feels the same.'

How was it that something you desperately wanted to hear could make you feel so awful, Jemma thought, as she reached for an overturned bucket and sat down, feeling that if she didn't, she might fall over.

Another Challenge Ahead

'Try slow, deep breaths,' Rosie said, crouching down beside Jemma, who was still perched on the upturned bucket. 'Finding out your crush fancies you can be a bit swoon inducing.'

Rosie's words cut through the fog that seemed to have settled on Jemma's brain and she forced herself to sit upright.

'I'm not swooning, Rosie. We aren't living in the nineteenth century!' Jemma shook her head, trying to convey disbelief and hide the fact that Rosie was uncomfortably near the mark. 'I'm just trying to recover some composure after experiencing a very public embarrassment.'

Jemma could see that Rosie looked both confused and more than a little unconvinced.

'Johnny Beckett, who thinks I am

secretly in love with Matt, decided that what the wildlife documentary needed was an uncomfortable and not to mention public, supposedly romantic lunch with my boss.'

Rosie was holding a hand over her mouth and doing a terrible job of holding back her giggles.

'I mean it's supposed to be about the pandas, for goodness' sake!'

'Well, in fairness, your lunch did seem to have the right effect on the bears. You have to admit that the behaviour we saw was very encouraging.'

Jemma sighed and nodded. She did have to concede that point although her memory of the lady commenting that the two incidents were related was still mortifying.

'Rosie, we are animal behaviourists. You're not seriously suggesting that the bears need to see Matt and me together as a couple, are you?' Jemma winced.

Seeing Matt and her as a couple was a dream, a private one but one that she now would need to work doubly hard to keep to herself.

'If you'd told me before today I would have laughed, but you have to admit that Bojing and Lijuan seem closer than they were. And besides, it's obvious that you fancy Matt and that you aren't going to do anything about it. So really, this is the best thing that could have happened.' Rosie smiled triumphantly.

'Rosie, I've told you, this was all set up by Beckett for the documentary,' Jemma said.

'Oh, come on, Jemma. You're not fooling me. I saw the way you looked at Matt when he took hold of your hand . . . '

Jemma stood up, deciding she had had quite enough of this conversation.

'All you saw,' she said, 'was me trying to work out how to eat my steak with only my fork.'

'Uh huh,' Rosie said as her eyes glittered mischievously. 'Well, even if I believe you, I know what I saw. Matt has a thing for you, too. I'm sure of it.'

Jemma turned away and started to tidy up the bench that was used to prepare the pandas' food. It wasn't exactly untidy, but it gave her something to do to distract her from the thought that Matt might have feelings for her.

Even if he did, he couldn't act on them, not with Betty in the picture. Or if he thought he could in his current circumstances he was going to get a nasty surprise. There was no way Jemma was going to be the other woman.

'And besides, I'm assuming that Johnny will want more of the same. After all, it seemed to be a hit with the visitors. I expect the viewing public will lap it up!' Rosie said.

'Well if you're so convinced that a romantic couple is the answer for the bears and the TV, why don't you and the gorgeous cameraman take over?' Jemma knew she sounded like a petulant teenager, but she couldn't help it. If Rosie was so convinced, why not put her own love life, not to mention reputation, on the line? After all, she was the one who seemed to enjoy being on camera.

'I did mention it to Johnny, but he said that all I wanted was a spring fling and that the viewers want something more,' Rosie said, and her expression had changed from amusement to introspection in a matter of seconds.

'I'm not sure I just want a spring fling,' Rosie added morosely. 'I mean you get to a stage in your life where you want the real thing, don't you? The person you know you are going to spend the rest of your life with. The one who doesn't mind if you get straight into your pyjamas as soon as you walk through the door after work.'

Jemma couldn't argue with that. Ever since she had had her heart broken, she had wondered if she would ever find the One. She had thrown herself into work and tried to ignore that part of her that wanted to love and be loved.

But then she had met Matt. She barely knew the man but somehow her heart had decided even when her head had said no. It was just saving up heartache, her head told her heart firmly. He wasn't hers to have, even if he did feel the same but deep-down Jemma knew there was more to it than that. Her trust had been shattered and she wasn't sure she would ever be ready to trust someone completely again.

Rosie was sighing and gazing off into the distance and Jemma thought that they had both had enough of romantic thoughts for one day. What they needed to do was get back to work. There was a whole schedule of animal care, not to mention interactive talks, which needed to be managed.

'Right, we need to get on,' Jemma said. 'Do you want to do the tiger talk at three or wash out the hippos?'

'I'll do the tiger talk,' Rosie said. Jemma smiled. She was not surprised that Rosie had chosen the talk. Rosie loved the hippos, as she did all the animals, but cleaning them out was a thankless task since as soon as they were let back in to their enclosure, they re-marked their territory, which meant that within minutes all your hard work was undone. Jemma didn't mind. In fact, being out of sight of the public was a much more appealing idea.

★   ★   ★

It took Jemma over an hour to wash out the wallowing tanks in the hippos' sleeping quarters and she was pink with the effort. Despite the overalls she had pulled on over her uniform she knew that she would carry the pungent smell of the hippos with her until she could throw her uniform in the washing machine at home and have a shower herself.

Having safely closed and locked the gates, she let the hippos have access to their sleeping quarters and Marla, the adult female, immediately dived back into the clear water and started about her business. Jemma laughed. That was all you could do, that and let the public know that the enclosures did get cleaned out daily and that the hippos were well cared for, despite appearances.

There was a knock on the inner door to the keepers' area and Jemma pulled the door open, wondering who had forgotten their key. She was surprised to see Matt standing there. In his expensive suit, he could not have looked more out of place.

'Ah, Jemma, Rosie said I'd find you here.'

The hour of cleaning had given Jemma the time to practise how she was going to behave when she saw Matt again and so she took a deep breath and smiled. Not a flirty, I-enjoyed-lunch kind of smile, but a professional, happy-to-speak-with-the-boss kind of smile.

'I like to get hands-on as much as I can,' Jemma said.

Matt glanced at the overalls and nodded.

'I can see that,' he said and then raised a hand to his nose.

'Perhaps we should talk outside? The hippos like to mark their territory,' Jemma said, smiling a little more broadly. It made a nice change for Matt to be the one who was out of his comfort zone.

'No, here is fine. I won't keep you long anyway. I just wanted to see if you were free tonight? Johnny has another scene he would like to shoot.'

Jemma had prepared herself for this and so nodded, as if the thought did not bother her at all.

'I can be, but won't Betty mind? Not that it's any of my business,' she added hurriedly. She was rewarded with a broad grin and Matt was clearly working his charm.

'Betty's pretty understanding, and I'll be sure to make it up to her.' He rubbed his hands together. 'Well, Johnny has asked for us to be back here for eight o'clock.'

'Right,' Jemma said. The only positive thing would be that the park shut at six and so at least there would be no public to watch the next stage of her embarrassment. No doubt the film crew would be there, but she would just have to put up with that.

'Great. I'll see you later. We are all

going to meet by the side gate,' Matt said. 'Have a good day.'

'Bye,' Jemma said, wishing, perhaps for the first time, that this Betty would put her foot down and demand that Matt spend less time at work. At least that would save her from whatever was to come later.

Romantic Gesture

Jemma had walked through her front door at a quarter past seven. The park might officially close at six, but Jemma rarely left when the public did. There was always something that needed to be sorted out before she left for the night.

The clock her grandma had given her chimed the half hour. Jemma sighed. If she didn't get off the sofa in the next ten minutes then she wouldn't have time to have a shower. Usually she came in and had a bath but tonight she didn't have time for her usual soak. Her phone pinged, and she looked at a message from Rosie.

'Brett says we are to wear formal dresses!' Jemma groaned. Getting dressed up with heels and make-up was something she rarely had the time or the energy for.

She forced herself off the sofa and

headed to her bedroom. She had a couple of posh dresses, which had been bought for weddings, but her choice would be limited.

Out of the shower and wrapped in a towel, she stared at her wardrobe. Both dresses were pretty and suited her figure so why did she feel so reluctant to pick one? Of course, deep down she knew why — she told herself as she glanced at her refection in the mirror that hung on the back of her bedroom door.

If she wore one of these she would look like she had made the effort to dress up, look like she was trying to impress someone. Trying to impress Matt. And that didn't sit well. Matt, after all, had a girlfriend and what if she gave him the wrong impression?

Jemma pulled on the dress that sat just below her knee. It was navy blue with sparkles around the V-neck and waist. She had loved it the moment she had tried it on in the shop.

She slipped it on and reached up a

hand to her hair, which was naturally curly, and tonight she had decided not to straighten it. Her reflection seemed to nod its approval and Jemma took that as a good sign.

She walked to her front door, picking up her bag. She had decided against the evening bag that she normally took with her when she was wearing the dress, that seemed a step too far.

With one hand on the front door handle, something was holding her back. It was a slightly sick feeling that had settled in her stomach. It took her a few moments to pin down exactly what it is was.

She didn't want to give Matt the wrong impression, that much was true, but there was another part of her which was worried that Matt wouldn't give her a second look, even though she was dressed up in her best outfit.

Being rejected because someone was in love with someone else was one thing, particularly if you had made a promise that you would never come between another couple. But how would she know that was the case? What if Matt simply wasn't interested? What if that had nothing to do with Betty?

She yanked the front door open and stepped through. You are never happy, she told herself firmly. Just don't give the wrong impression yourself. That's the only thing you can control.

The staff car park had a few cars in it and the TV crew van was also parked up. There was no sign of anyone, so Jemma could only assume they had arrived early to get set up. She used her pass to buzz herself in through the first gate. At the inner gate, Jeff, the night security guard, waved and let her through.

'Well, don't you look lovely this evening?' Jeff said with twinkling eyes. Jeff had worked at the park since it opened, and Jemma had a soft spot for him. He reminded her of her grandpa.

'Feels a bit strange to be dressed up for work. I'm so used to wearing my uniform.'

'Well, you look magnificent and it's

nice to see you without the ridiculous hat.' Jeff grinned, and Jemma grinned back.

'And besides, lassie, it will all be worth it.' Jeff looked as if he knew something that Jemma didn't but one glance at her watch told her if she didn't get a move on she would be late.

She had been sure the plan was to meet at the gate but since no-one else was there, apart from Jeff, she walked through the park and headed towards the panda enclosure.

It was the lights she saw first. The sky was dark, and she could just about make out the stars, but these stars seemed much closer to earth. Someone, the TV crew perhaps, had strung a net of tiny soft white fairy lights above the viewing platform for the pandas.

There was music, too, and Jemma realised that it wasn't anything as mundane as a CD player. Off to one side, dressed all in black, was a string quartet. She blinked as she tried to work out exactly what was going on. What was

Johnny Beckett up to?

She spotted Rosie, dressed in a floor-length gown, with her hair piled expertly up on the top of her head, and scurried towards her. The crew seemed to be setting up a range of cameras around the area. Clearly, they did not want to miss a moment.

'Isn't it amazing?' Rosie gushed. 'So romantic!'

'Yes, I suppose,' Jemma said, still staring at the musicians. Rosie gave her a disapproving glance and Jemma felt a slight pang of guilt. Rosie was right, of course, someone had gone to a huge amount of effort.

'But why?' Jemma asked Rosie. She wasn't sure why she expected Rosie to know, but these days she always seemed to be one step ahead of her.

'Johnny wanted to do something romantic so we're going to pretend it's a staff event. You know, a dinner and dance,' Rosie said, as if that explained it all.

'OK, but why here, near the bears? Is

he expecting the bears to start waltz-ing?' Jemma felt like she had travelled to an alien world where all the rules were different.

'No, silly.' Rosie rolled her eyes. 'It's a wildlife documentary, remember?'

Jemma sighed. As if she could forget that. But it still didn't really make sense to her.

'Johnny wanted to show the park out of hours. You know, an event to show that the staff at the park are more of a family.'

Jemma scanned around her but she could only see herself and Rosie. That didn't seem much like a staff event.

'But where are the rest of us?' Jemma asked but she had a sinking feeling that she knew where they all were. At home, with their feet up, watching TV.

'Well, that's the most exciting bit!' Rosie said, jumping up and down and clapping her hands, like a kid on Christmas Eve.

'It's going to play out like you thought it was a staff event but really it's just Matt surprising you with a date. So romantic!' Rosie gushed.

'Right,' Jemma said. She was starting to get a headache again, or maybe it was just the awful sense of foreboding. It was one thing to keep Matt at arm's length at a dance with lots of other people, but it was going to be much harder when it was just the two of them. Jemma sighed. That wasn't it at all, of course. What she was worried about was whether her decision to stay away from Matt was going to withstand an overwhelmingly romantic gesture.

Lost to the World

Jemma was trying to work out what she was going to do when the quartet came to a loud conclusion. Each of the four nodded their heads as if they were bowing to an audience.

'Rosie, darling? Can you let the bears out?' Johnny said and Jemma watched as Rosie rushed off, in through the keepers' door. A minute later there was the sound of grinding metal and the doors to the pandas' sleeping quarters were opened.

Jemma watched and waited but no pandas appeared. They were so used to spending the nights in their sleeping quarters that she wondered if the whole dance show would be for nothing.

Perhaps if they refused to come out, the TV crew wouldn't bother to include the footage in the documentary? That was the first cheery thought that Jemma had had all evening.

The TV crew had all cameras on the panda enclosure but after ten minutes Jemma could see that they were getting a little restless. Suddenly the idea arose that she might be able to go home and have that soak in the bath after all.

'Can we have some music?' Johnny asked, and the quartet smoothly started to play ballroom dance music.

Jemma stared at the ground and hoped that someone else would dance, although who, she didn't know. Maybe Rosie and her cameraman, if he could be persuaded to give up his camera? Jemma knew she had two left feet.

'Let the dancing begin!' Johnny said with a flourish.

Jemma risked a glance upwards and realised that his command was directed at Matt, who seemed to have appeared from nowhere. He was wearing a black tuxedo, white shirt and black bow-tie and he managed to look both classic and classy.

Matt's eyes settled on Jemma and for a split second she thought his eyes went wide as he took in what she was wearing. Jemma could feel the heat start to rise in her chest and could only hope that she had put on enough make-up to disguise her blooming blush.

Matt walked across the space between them, his shiny black shoes clicking on the concrete. He held out a hand to Jemma and smiled.

'May I have this dance?' he asked.

Jemma felt like real life had merged with her recent dreams — except in her dreams she could dance every step with elegance and beauty. She had a worrying feeling that this was going to quickly turn into a nightmare.

Matt tilted his head to one side and Jemma wondered if he could read her mind. He wiggled the fingers on the hand he held out to her and so she took it, not knowing what else to do. With ease, Matt pulled her into his arms.

'Relax, Jemma. Just follow my lead.'

Matt moved his right foot and whispered in to her ear.

'Left foot forward.'

Jemma did as she was told. It wasn't exactly smooth but at least she hadn't fallen over or stepped on Matt's highly polished shoes. Matt smiled at her.

'Now your right foot forward. Right foot joins your left and then left foot back. Right foot back.'

Jemma managed to follow this and almost felt like she was dancing.

'You've got it,' he whispered softly, and Jemma was hopeful that no-one else could hear his impromptu dance lesson. 'We'll keep going like this but move around the space, just follow me.'

Jemma was concentrating so hard that she was sure she was frowning but as the music played and Matt whirled her expertly around she could feel herself start to relax.

'That's great, Jemma, now if you could smile a little. You know? Pretend like you are enjoying yourself,' Johnny said, his voice coming from off camera.

Jemma could feel herself stiffen at the words, which were meant in jest but cut deep and Matt swirled her around so that her face was hidden from the cameras.

'You're doing brilliantly, Jemma. Just pretend that they aren't there,' Matt said, and his smile was so encouraging that Jemma's heart skipped a beat.

Matt's eyes seemed to draw her in and so she focused on his face and found that her feet were obeying the rhythm of the dance without any conscious thought.

The pace of the music seemed to slow and then fade out and Jemma wished that it would continue. She felt lost to the world, dancing with Matt and although she knew that others were there with them, watching them closely, she still felt as if the world contained only her and Matt. Deep down she knew it couldn't last, that it couldn't be that way for ever, but that didn't stop her from wishing.

There was silence as the music faded, as if no-one wanted to break the spell that had been cast.

'Look!' a voice said softly into the

silence. Jemma was pretty sure it was Rosie. Matt still held Jemma in one arm and so he spun them both round so that they were facing the panda enclosure.

At some point the pandas had appeared from their sleeping enclosures and were sitting together on one of the highest rocks staring out at the humans. For a split second, Jemma felt like they were the animals and the pandas were the people who had come to see the humans in their natural environment. Both pandas tilted their heads to one side as if they were trying to work out what was going on.

'Brett, a shot of the pandas, if you please?' Johnny said, keeping his voice soft. 'Then back to the dancers,' he directed.

Jemma had lost track of time as she had been whirled around the dance floor by Matt. The music had changed but Matt led her through the steps. Jemma didn't want the night to end but after a while both she and Matt were breathing quite hard.

'I could do with a drink,' Matt said, his cheeks looking a little pink.

'Me too,' Jemma said as Matt spun her out so that she was at arm's length. He bowed and then held out an arm. Jemma took it and then paraded them to a small table which had been set up and contained tall stemmed glasses of what looked like champagne. Matt poured her a glass.

'My treat,' he said, handing it over. 'And don't worry, we'll get taxis home.' He grinned and raised his own glass to Jemma's and they chinked them together.

In Jemma's dream she had thought about how it would be to go on a proper date with Matt and even though she knew this wasn't really a date, it felt wonderful.

The moment was broken by a beeping sound from Matt's pocket.

'Probably Betty,' Matt said with a grin. 'I'll just check up on her and I'll be right back.'

Jemma tried to smile. It was a good thing that Betty had interrupted, as

Jemma felt like she was in danger of falling properly in love and that would be no good for her or Matt.

She remembered how she felt when she discovered that her boyfriend had been seeing someone else at the same time as her. Aside from the hurt and shame, there was also anger. She had been angry at herself for failing to see the signs but also that her ex-boyfriend had betrayed her in such a manner.

Jemma thought of Matt and realised that part of her was angry with him, too. He probably thought he was doing nothing wrong, that it was just some harmless flirting, but Jemma knew only too well the pain that it could cause Betty, not to mention herself.

Jemma knew what she needed to do. She needed to put an end to this here and now. She still wasn't entirely sure what 'this' was but she knew deep down that any joy and excitement she experienced now would pale in comparison to the pain and shame she might feel later, especially if she let herself play any role in coming between another couple. Jemma walked over to Rosie and handed over her nearly full glass of champagne.

'I need to go home,' she said to Rosie who looked surprised and then shocked.

'Is everything all right?' Rosie said, her face now showing concern.

Jemma nodded. This wasn't the moment to explain.

'I just really need to go home. Are you OK to ensure the pandas are back in their sleeping pens and everything is locked up?'

'Of course. Jemma, are you sure . . . '

Jemma didn't hear the end of the sentence as she started to walk away. Once she was sure that she was out of sight, she pulled off her heels and ran. She thought she heard Matt calling her name but pushed the thought away. He was no doubt still talking to Betty and Jemma's imagination was just playing a cruel trick on her.

Jemma was relieved that the security booth was empty. Jeff was obviously out on his hourly rounds. She pulled her ID from her bag and buzzed herself through both doors. Jeff had left some of the car park lights on and so Jemma was able to see her car, parked where she had left it, across the shingle.

Jemma wanted to keep on running, to jump in her car and speed home and then hide under the duvet, possibly for ever, but one bare foot on the shingle told her that she needed to put her shoes back on. She moaned in frustration, worried perhaps that Matt would chase after her. With her shoes back on she made her way quickly to her car and climbed in.

As she turned on the engine, her headlights came on and lit up the staff entrance. There was no sign of anyone, not Jeff and not Matt. She knew that she should be glad. Surely if he didn't chase after her, that had to be a sign that to him at least, nothing was going on? The problem was, all she felt was bitter disappointment.

Bemused and Confused

When Jemma woke up the next morning, for a split second she thought it had all been a dream. A dream that started out wonderfully and ended up with deep disappointment and heart-ache.

Sitting up in bed, Jemma could see her beautiful navy dress cast aside over the small armchair that sat in the corner of her bedroom. She could also see her shoes that she had kicked off and knew that however much she wished it, last night was not a dream. As her mind started to replay the events of the night before, Jemma collapsed on her bed and closed her eyes.

Dancing with Matt had been wonderful. She had truly felt as if no-one else was there. It was just her and Matt and the music. For a short while she had been able to imagine what it would be like if Matt loved her, what it would be like if Matt didn't already have a partner. But she hadn't been able to ignore the facts or the promise she had once made herself and so she had run away.

All she had needed to do was leave one of her shoes behind and she would have been Cinderella, running away before the dream disappeared at midnight. Jemma groaned at the thought and covered her face with a pillow.

She was going to have to get up and face them. Rosie was going to want to know what on earth last night was all about and that was before she could even think about Matt.

It might have been her imagination, but she was sure that she had heard Matt calling her name. Matt would be, at best, confused; and at worst, hurt by her leaving. For a moment she wondered if she should lie, make up some kind of emergency that might reasonably explain her behaviour, but she knew that she couldn't.

For one thing, her face would give it away. She was a terrible liar and even if she could manage to sound convincing her flushed cheeks would show that it was all made up. And besides she was just avoiding the inevitable. She needed to have a conversation with Matt. She needed to explain that she couldn't even think of a relationship with him, not if he already had a girlfriend.

Jemma threw off the pillow and kicked off the duvet. She swung her legs to the floor and walked determinedly in the direction of a shower. She had made up her mind, she was going to confront Matt. Tell him that she wasn't interested in him if he was with Betty and so they needed to go back to having a purely professional relation-ship.

It was only when she was getting dressed in her uniform and pulling on her furry hat that she wondered if the change she had felt in their relationship had in fact all been in her head?

What if Matt was bemused and

confused? What if he only saw her as a colleague and possibly a friend? Could she risk the mortification of seeing Matt first confused and then embarrassed as he had to explain to her what was really going on, at least from his point of view?

Jemma always looked forward to work. Some days she still couldn't believe that she was getting paid for doing something that she loved so much. But today she almost wished she could call in sick. She wouldn't, of course — the animals still needed her care and her time, however she was feeling.

She took a deep breath as she swiped her card and walked through the staff entrance. She was early which was good. Hopefully she could get on with work and maybe even avoid people, or at least Matt.

Jemma did her usual early morning walk around, inspecting the enclosures, making sure that there was no damage before the animals were allowed out to stretch their respective legs and more importantly, do a head count.

There wasn't anything more likely to mean a withdrawal of licence than animal escape. Standing outside the lion sleeping quarters, she ticked off the last box on her check list. All of the big mammals were accounted for. It was harder to keep tabs on the smaller mammals as they were harder to spot but a missing lion was not going to go unnoticed by the public.

'All present and correct?' The voice made Jemma jump as she was sure that she locked the outer gates behind her. 'A missing creature would really spice things up.'

Jemma turned and found a camera in her face. Johnny was standing there looking at the lions thoughtfully. Jemma felt cross that her morning peace had been disrupted, cross that the camera crew had come in to the lion area when they were supposed to be making a documentary about the pandas.

And that was before she thought about what would happen to one of her lions if someone was careless enough to allow them to escape.

'We have tried and tested protocols to prevent that happening.' Jemma glared at the camera. 'I think we can probably all agree that it would not be good news for the lion.' Jemma turned her glare on Johnny. It was the expression she usually saved for the lowest of the low in her book, people who were cruel to animals. Johnny didn't even seem to notice, and Jemma wondered if he was used to getting that kind of reaction in his line of work.

'Can I ask what you are doing? Your permits don't cover you to be here.'

'Just thought we would get some background shots. You know, some fillers in case we need them.'

'You are welcome to take as many filler shots as you like, as long as you remain in the public access areas.' Jemma held up her arm in the direction of the exit. When neither the camera crew nor Johnny showed any signs of moving on, Jemma took a step towards them and moved them to the exit, much like a sheepdog rounding up sheep.

Once they were all outside, Jemma made a show of triple locking the door.

Johnny looked unimpressed and Jemma wondered if they were about to fall out.

'I'm sure if I spoke to Matt, he would be happy to authorise full access, this documentary being so important to the park's future,' Johnny remarked.

The emphasis on 'the park's future' was not lost on Jemma and she could feel her cheeks start to colour.

'Unfortunately, you would also need my sign off, as I am the manager for the large mammal section,' Jemma said. She felt like she had agreed to enough already and besides, the lions had potential to cause serious harm, unlike the pandas who were fairly low risk.

'We'll see about that,' Johnny said confidently.

Jemma merely raised an eyebrow in a kind of silent challenge. She hadn't been sure about this man when she first met him and now she was beginning to feel that she really didn't like him much. Johnny was too focused on his project to see that the animals' needs should always come first.

'Good morning. I'm glad that I caught you both.'

Jemma hadn't noticed Matt's approach and she wondered how much of the conversation he had overheard. She didn't feel at all prepared to see him for the first time but on reflection an audience would help. He couldn't really get into anything personal with Johnny and his camera crew around.

'Morning, Mattie-boy. How goes things?' Johnny's smile was dazzling, and Jemma was sure she had never seen him be so matey with Matt.

'I'm very well, thank you. I wanted to ask you how the shoot from last night came out?'

Johnny slapped Matt and the back and leaned in conspiratorially.

'You were simply marvellous. Your dancing was brilliant, and you always come across so well on film. You know you could have a future in television presenting if you ever get fed up of your work here.'

Matt smiled his usual smile and Jemma wondered if Johnny was right, if Matt would agree to extend their access. Jemma watched them walk away, before Matt turned and looked back over his shoulder.

'I need to catch up with you, too, Jemma. Can we meet in my office at twelve?'

'Of course,' Jemma replied, but having the distinct impression that her answer was lost amidst all Johnny's enthusiasm.

Jemma did what she always did when life felt overwhelming — she threw herself into work. Keeping herself busy seemed to do the trick.

At five to twelve, Jemma walked up to the management offices and made her way to Matt's secretary. His door was standing open and even from where Jemma was standing she could see that he was not in his office.

'Mr Darnell's not in,' Tina said,

smiling up at her kindly. 'Did you have an appointment?' she asked.

'Matt asked me to come and meet him in his office at twelve.'

'He's gone out for lunch. Mr Beckett invited him to the pub.'

'Fair enough,' Jemma said and forced a smile on to her face, even though she was feeling anything but happy. 'I'll try to catch him later.'

'I'll let him know that you were here.' Tina frowned. 'He's usually pretty good at remembering his day's appointments.'

'Not to worry,' Jemma said, trying to inject a light-hearted tone to her words. 'It wasn't exactly an official meeting and I'm sure it's not urgent.'

Jemma was annoyed, she had a right to be. He had wanted to meet at 12 and she had taken time out of her busy working day to walk up to the offices and he didn't even have the decency to remember.

It seemed that Johnny and the money that came with the documentary had stronger charms than Jemma had imagined. But then maybe that was a good thing. It wasn't like she wanted to see Matt just now. She still hadn't worked out how she was going to explain her mysterious disappearance, at least not without giving away her heart.

True Colours

Jemma didn't see Matt all afternoon and that gave her the time to practise her nonchalance. If he apologised for not being at the office, then she would wave it away as if it were nothing. If he didn't mention the fact that he had basically stood her up, then she wasn't about to bring it up, either. Cool, calm and collected was the name of the game.

At six o'clock the park shut its gates and security started their final sweep to ensure that no stragglers would be left in the park overnight. Jemma had been half waiting for Matt to appear all day, but the waiting was starting to wear down her new approach of calm and collected.

All she could think was that Matt had taken the whole afternoon off to hang out with his new best friend, Johnny

Beckett. She wondered if he had done it because he knew that Jemma wasn't keen on the man — or was he just that desperate to avoid her? He needn't be, she thought to herself. She had no plans to let anything happen between them.

Jemma closed down her computer in the small office which also served as the break room for the large mammal keepers and decided to call it a night. Perhaps Matt would come and find her tomorrow. One thing she was sure of was that she wasn't going to go out of her way to seek him out.

She had plenty of work to be getting on with. The park was due its annual inspection in the next month and so it was important that all the paperwork was up to scratch as well as all the enclosures. Jemma grabbed her bag and walked out of the door, turning to lock it.

'Ah, Jemma, I'm glad I've tracked you down at last.'

Jemma took her time locking the

door. The cheek of the man! She had been exactly where she was supposed to be all day. It wasn't as if she was the one who had forgotten their scheduled meeting. She took a moment to compose her face and then turned to face Matt. He had shed both his suit jacket and his tie and looked like he had enjoyed his afternoon off immensely.

'I'm sorry I missed you earlier,' he said, flashing Jemma a smile.

Personally, Jemma didn't think he had 'missed' her. He had simply decided that going out for a lunchtime drink with Johnny was more important, but she reminded herself of her new approach and held her tongue, on that point at least.

'No problem, I know you're very busy,' Jemma said, hoping that it wouldn't sound sarcastic. Matt seemed to take the comment at face value and didn't look at all embarrassed, so he clearly thought that he had done nothing wrong.

And now here he was being all nice. Was he trying to win her over? The very idea made her cross, not just for herself but for Betty as well. Jemma knew how it felt to be in the dark, when everyone else around you knew what was going on and with that thought came a sudden burst of anger.

'And what about poor Betty?' Jemma said fiercely before clenching both fists and staring at the ground. This was not the plan, not the plan at all. If only he had come and found her earlier. Earlier she would have been able to stick to her plan, but she had had too much time to work herself up to being angry and now she had said something she shouldn't. Matt for his part looked bemused.

'I'm sorry?' he said, trying out a smile but Jemma didn't return it and his face dropped as if he had been told Christmas had been cancelled.

'What's Betty got to do with . . . ' Matt stopped. He didn't seem to know what was going on and so had no idea how to finish his sentence. Jemma glared at him. Playing dumb was not cutting it with her. He must know that what he was doing was wrong, even if he wasn't prepared to admit it to her and his act wasn't fooling her.

'You remember Betty?' Jemma said icily. She knew that the anger she was feeling was coming from the past and that the person she was really angry at wasn't here. She had never been able to say any of this to her ex. She had been so shocked and hurt that she had told him she never wanted to see him again, and never had.

'I'm wondering why you do.' Matt's expression was serious but still betrayed that he wasn't sure what was going on.

'Does Betty know what you get up to when you're not at home with her?' Jemma felt like it was time to cut through the nonsense and get to the point.

Now that she had started this she figured she might as well point out the facts to Matt. Who knew, maybe he would see the error of his ways and she could save Betty some of the heartache she had experienced.

Now Matt looked more amused than

anything and that only fired up Jemma's indignation. How could he think that was funny? She had thought that she had known Matt, she had felt that he was one of the good guys but now, showing such a lack of concern for his girlfriend that she was sure that he was cut from the same cloth as her ex.

'The fact that you find that amusing is enough for me to end this conversation,' Jemma said, knowing that she sounded haughty.

She had had enough. All she wanted to do was put some distance between her and Matt. Matt seemed to have finally shown his true colours and she needed to get away to think. To adjust her idea of who Matt was.

If she could do that then maybe she could let go of the dreams her mind had created. Maybe then she could move on. She would be civil, he was her boss after all, but no more.

Matt seemed to have lost the power of speech and Jemma almost felt sorry for him. There was something about his look that made her feel like perhaps he didn't understand that what he was doing was wrong.

She opened her mouth to speak but then closed it again. She had said enough — now he needed to go away and think about her words and his behaviour.

'I need to go,' Jemma said.

'Goodnight,' she called out as she turned to walk swiftly away.

'Jemma, wait . . . ' he called, and she could hear him take a few steps to follow her. In response she sped up.

'Jemma?' Then his footsteps stopped. Jemma hurried on, taking the shortest route to the staff entrance. Once she was through it she ran for her car, as if she were being chased.

Jemma drove home with the conversation replaying in her head. Her mind seemed determined to examine every word and gesture.

Once indoors she kicked off her shoes before putting the kettle on. Thinking about it, she decided, wasn't going to change what had just happened. In fact, she was in danger of building it up to much worse, so she forced the thoughts from her mind.

She reached for her laptop. In her free time she had been working on a book, which she hoped one day to publish, about the care of pandas in captivity. Her passion for animals would surely be enough to keep her mind occupied.

After a bath and wrapped in her dressing gown, Jemma sat on her sofa with her laptop on her knees and stared at the blank page. The cursor seemed to flash accusingly at her lack of progress. It reminded her of the past when she had been too worn out with emotion to do anything other than the basic functions of life. For months she felt like she was sleep walking through her life, caught up in a haze of pain and sadness.

But she had found her way back, thrown herself back in to the job that she loved, and she wasn't about to let another man take that from her again.

The worst that Matt could be accused of was raising her hopes that she might have found love again and perhaps that was all down to her anyway. Maybe it had all been in her head and he had truly been oblivious? But whatever the case she was not going to let it happen again.

If there had ever been a chance for her and Matt, it was gone now. Aside from the issue of Betty, Matt had shown that he wasn't the man for her and she clearly wasn't the woman for him.

Now that she had made the decision, she needed to move on, to think about something else. Think about her book. But she couldn't think what to write and so she let her mind replay all that had happened since Johnny and his film crew had arrived.

Her tutor at university had once told her that if you have writer's block you should try to write about anything — anything that would get words down on paper. It didn't matter if the words were irrelevant — you could always delete them later — but somehow the act of writing something could often get the creative juices going.

And so Jemma rested her fingers on the keyboard and started to record everything that had happened. All the unexpected changes in the pandas' behaviour and the ridiculous theories that Rosie, Matt and the awful Johnny seemed to support — that somehow seeing Matt and her play at romance had given the pandas the prompt they needed to bond.

She had no intention of leaving any of that in her book, but it felt good to be writing something. Even if it was about the ridiculous things that had happened to her since Matt and the film crew had walked into her life.

Impossible Dream?

Surprisingly, Jemma felt pretty good, despite the fact that she hadn't managed much sleep. It hadn't been dreams and regrets that had kept her awake, it had been the typing.

Once she started to record all the events that had happened since Matt's arrival, she found she couldn't stop and had written thousands of words, finally stopping in the early hours when she reached the end of the story so far.

What had surprised her most was her observations of the change in the bears' behaviour. There had certainly been a defrosting of relations, but she wasn't prepared to give Rosie's mad theory credit for it just yet.

Her team had put months of hard work into the care of the pandas and making sure their environment was as close to natural as possible. Surely that had more to do with it than her and Matt pretending to be in love? If nothing else, it left her in a thoughtful mood as she made her way to work.

Rosie was in bright and early but then so was the film crew which seemed to bode well for Jemma's new approach.

'Morning,' Jemma said to the little crowd, 'I was going to watch some of the CCTV footage from the last few nights to see if I can pick up any promising signs. Might be good for the show,' Jemma said, directing her last comment to Johnny, who looked as surprised at the verbal olive branch as did the rest of the crew, not to mention Rosie.

'Great,' Johnny said, rubbing his hands together as if it had all been his idea. He was looking at Jemma curiously but she was careful not to catch his eye.

'If we view it in the staff break room we should have enough room for all of us,' Jemma said, smiling.

She started to walk in the direction of the break room and could hear the crew hoisting cameras on to shoulders as they hurried after her. It felt good to be focusing on work, focusing on what was really important and Jemma put her good mood, which was as much a surprise to herself as it was to everyone else, down to that.

Jemma sat in front of the small elderly TV screen and pressed play. She had decided to watch the footage from the previous night first and then work backwards. The cameraman, Brett, was standing beside her, but his focus seemed to be the screen itself, which was all right by Jemma. Aside from anything else, this was how documentaries, serious documentaries, were supposed to be conducted. Not filming two people dance in a vain attempt to teach mammals about love and romance.

A hush fell over the room as a grainy black and white image filled the screen. It showed the two bears sleeping and nothing else. Jemma pressed the button to wind on the footage and then paused it, before pressing play again.

'What are they doing?' Johnny asked

sounding a little in awe of what he was seeing.

'They're building a nest,' Jemma said unable to take her eyes from the screen.

'Hah!' Johnny said. 'I knew it! This documentary is going to be golden! And if we throw in a panda cub for good measure we might even win some awards.'

Jemma felt all eyes on her. Apparently no-one else was that bothered about the idea of awards, they were more interested in whether a cub was in the pandas' future.

'It's not definitive but it's a good sign.' The first real sign, Jemma thought, that a panda cub might not be an impossible dream.

'They're working together,' Rosie said, 'I've never seen them willingly share the same space, let alone . . . ' When Jemma looked up at her, Rosie had tears in her eyes.

'I can't believe that it worked! All they needed to do was have someone to model their behaviour on,' Rosie added.

Jemma allowed herself a wry smile.

Somehow, she doubted that was the case but in the end, she wasn't sure it really mattered. To breed panda bears successfully in captivity outside of China was rare, and maybe, just maybe, they had managed it.

'Did I hear the word cub?' A voice sounded from the open door.

'You certainly did, Mattie boy! It looks as if the pandas may be preparing for the pitter-patter of tiny panda feet.'

'Really?' Matt asked, and he sounded pleased.

'We're looking at the CCTV footage from last night,' Jemma said, wondering why she felt the need to gain some perceived ground back from Johnny. He had stolen her thunder and it wasn't as if he had made any contribution to the care of the pandas. Not that any of that really mattered since it looked as if she might have achieved her lifelong goal.

'Does it show something?' Matt asked, prompting Jemma from her self-reflection, but before she could speak Johnny was off.

'It looks as if the pandas are building a kind of nest, possibly for baby pandas!' Johnny said, turning to the camera that Brett had focused in on his face. Johnny showed two thumbs up and grinned madly at the camera before turning to Matt and steering him to a position behind the screen.

'Would you mind, Jemma? We'd like to get some shots of Matt watching the footage for the first time?' Johnny said, nice as pie.

Jemma did mind, as much as she tried not to. It wasn't that she wanted to be on the TV, particularly in this kind of reality TV documentary, but still. She wanted the public to learn something about pandas, something factual. She doubted that Matt would have much insight to offer to the bears' behaviour and what it might mean.

Jemma got up from her seat and Matt slipped into it, his eyes fixed on the screen.

'Make sure you get tight in on Matt's face,' Johnny instructed Brett. 'I want to capture his reaction. Then we can cut that with a copy of the actual footage from the CCTV.'

Jemma decided that she had better things to do with her time than to stand around and watch them filming. For one thing she wanted to share the news with the rest of the large mammal crew and for another she needed some space to fix her new attitude back in place.

She was sure the reason she had reacted to Johnny's behaviour was just a throwback to how she used to feel, and she wasn't about to let that happen again.

★   ★   ★

'You're like the Scarlet Pimpernel!'

In fact, Jemma had seen Matt walking up the narrow path that led to the keepers' shed behind the lion enclosure and so she had plenty of time to plan her response.

'Sorry. Did you need me for something?' she asked, pleased that her voice remained even and appropriate for a conversation between a worker and her boss.

She put down her clipboard which she was using to stocktake the lion food in the big chest freezer and looked in his direction.

'Great news about the pandas,' Matt said, grinning widely, and Jemma had to look away, worried that if she stared at his smiling face for too long her reserve might melt.

'It is but we need to be cautious. We don't actually know if Lijuan is pregnant.' Jemma kept a smile on her face. She didn't want to ruin his mood but felt she needed to point out the facts of the matter.

'I understand but it's still a step forward. And Johnny got some great footage. He seems really pleased.'

'I'm sure he was,' Jemma said, in what she hoped was a gracious tone.

'You and your team have worked incredibly hard but Johnny's suggestion for the extra angle to the documentary seems to have taken us to the next step.'

'Let's hope so.'

Matt raised his eyebrows and Jemma wondered if he was surprised by her reaction.

'I think he is probably planning his final scheme,' Matt said. 'I know his presence hasn't been easy for you, but I think we can both agree that if we get a cub out of this then it will all of have been worth it — not to mention the additional funding and hike in visitor numbers.'

Jemma was surprised that Matt had remembered the correct term and smiled. To be fair, he had done everything that Johnny had asked of him too, and some of that can't have been easy for him, either. Jemma felt her resolve slip a little at this latest information, but she pushed it aside firmly.

She had made up her mind about the possibility of a relationship with Matt and she had been happier since.

There was no way back, not in her mind anyway. There was Betty to consider and besides all that, Matt didn't seem to be interested in a relationship with Jemma.

'Well, it certainly hasn't been what I expected from a wildlife documentary but I can manage one more stunt if you can?' Jemma smiled but Matt didn't return it.

She got the impression he was studying her closely and maybe even that he was trying to work her out and not having much luck.

'Do you know when it might be?' Jemma asked, feeling uncomfortable in the silence and wanting to shake Matt from his contemplation.

'Matt?' she queried when he said nothing.

'Sorry,' he said, shaking his head, 'I've no idea but I imagine it will be soon. Johnny and the crew will be wrapping up next week.'

'Are you OK?' Jemma asked the question before she could talk herself out of it. She shouldn't ask. She should just pretend nothing was going on, that they were having a perfectly normal conversation, but the question slipped out.

'Fine, just . . . ' Matt seemed

reluctant to verbalise his thoughts. Jemma waited.

⋆ ⋆ ⋆

Having asked the question she thought that she should at least give him the opportunity to answer, even if she wasn't sure she wanted to know.

'I wanted to ask you about the other night.'

Jemma nodded but fought to keep her expression neutral.

'I wanted to ask why you rushed off so suddenly — you know, on the night of the dance?'

'Oh, that, yes . . . kind of embarrassing. My shoes were hurting,' Jemma said. It was true in the sense that her shoes were not designed for dancing for that length of time and had started to pinch a little. It wasn't the reason why she left, of course, but she didn't want to try and explain that, either.

She watched as Matt nodded slowly. She wondered if he was going to ask her why she had run off, why she hadn't said goodbye or even stopped when he called after her but the look on his face in that moment suggested that he didn't want to hear the answer any more than Jemma wanted to tell him the truth.

'Right, fair enough. Well, I'll let you get back to work and I expect I will see you again when Johnny has decided what he wants us to do next.'

Matt turned on his heel, muttering his goodbyes and then he was gone.

A Waiting Game

Rosie bounced into the hippo keeper area as Jemma was finishing sorting out the barrel of food.

'I have some amazing news,' Rosie said, hopping from foot to foot.

'You've won the lottery?' Jemma asked, smiling at her younger colleague.

Rosie snorted and waved that comment aside.

'No, it's about Johnny!' Rosie said, clapping her hands with unconcealed excitement.

'Hollywood are calling him and he has to leave?' Jemma asked innocently, knowing that she was having a bit of a dig at the man, who probably wasn't as bad as Jemma thought. Rosie stopped clapping and frowned.

'The crew will be packing up next week. Brett says he's not sure where they'll be filming next. Could be anywhere,' Rosie said, suddenly sounding morose. Jemma felt a little stab of guilt.

'Oh, well hopefully we'll have something exciting to look forward to,' Jemma said, her eyes lighting up at the thought.

'It's so frustrating not knowing and having to wait and see if one day there's a cub.'

'Well we can try and collect dung specimens again but we both know that's not particularly accurate.'

'And we don't want to do anything that might upset Lijuan,' Rosie said thoughtfully. 'We would have to separate them to make sure we had the right sample.'

'It's surprising to think that separating them might upset them after all the time they wouldn't go near each other, but I think we're better off playing the waiting game.' Ultimately it was Jemma's decision and she had made it. Patience was a virtue, after all.

'Um,' Rosie said, agreeing. 'Still frustrating, though.'

'Such is the life of a keeper,' Jemma said. 'Anyway, you came here to tell me about Johnny?'

'Yes, yes, of course. Well, Johnny wants to show the family side of the park.'

Rosie looked so excited, but Jemma could only imagine what that would mean for her and Matt.

'And how do we go about doing that?' Jemma asked even though she didn't really want to know the answer.

'Johnny has arranged to borrow a baby.'

Jemma blinked, sure that she had misheard.

'I'm sorry — he's done what?' Jemma could feel the all too familiar panic rising inside her. Where on earth had Johnny Beckett 'borrowed' a baby from?

'He's borrowing a baby. You know Jane from the gift shop?'

'Yes,' Jemma said slowly, hoping once more this was all a terrible dream.

'Well, Johnny asked her if he could borrow her baby, told her that her baby would be a little star in the documentary.

He thinks it will play well with the viewers. You know, you and Matt with a baby and the pandas preparing to have a cub.'

'Rosie. The pandas are surrounded by families all day long. I think we've got that covered,' Jemma said the words slowly, hoping that Rosie would understand how crazy the idea sounded.

'Yes, but you have to admit that all that Johnny has asked you to do so far has been good for the bears.'

Jemma shook her head wondering if she was the person who wasn't getting it.

'Rosie, they've seen us eat lunch and dance.' Jemma's mind prickled with the memory of being swirled around in Matt's arms as he taught her to dance. She tried to brush it aside. That was the last thing she wanted to be thinking about right now. She needed to concentrate.

'I very much doubt that has anything to do with it.'

'You don't know that for sure. And besides Johnny says it creates a great juxtaposition on film for the viewers.'

Jemma seriously doubted that any of the viewers would be interested in the 'juxtaposition of images' and sighed.

'How on earth will we explain the sudden appearance of a baby?' Jemma said, trying to be reasonable.

'Simple. Johnny is going to explain that you have been asked to care for the baby. He thinks it will soften your image with the viewers.'

Jemma stared. Since she had met Johnny he had seemed capable of insulting her in lots of different ways. The only thing that could be said about this comment was the fact that Rosie didn't seem to consider it an insult.

'And it won't hurt for Bojing and Lijuan to see you modelling parenting behaviour.'

Personally, Jemma thought that they would be relying on the pandas' natural instincts to kick in — assuming there would be a panda cub to parent.

'Rosie, you and I both know that it's not definite that Lijuan is pregnant.'

'You yourself said there have been

lots of promising signs. And I thought you said that you would do anything to help the pandas?' Rosie raised an eyebrow in silent challenge.

Rosie was right, of course, not to mention the fact that she had agreed to take part in the documentary for the park's sake . . . but still. Was this whole debacle really necessary?

'Fine.' At least it would be her last time on camera, Jemma thought. 'When are we borrowing this baby?'

'Tomorrow morning. Matt has given Jane the day off so she's going to bring her children to the park. She'll take them off and play whilst you and Matt look after the baby.'

Jemma, whose parenting experience was limited to holding a friend's baby once, could only hope that Matt knew more than she did. Otherwise, she was sure that the only thing they would achieve would be to convince pandas that the humans shouldn't be allowed to raise their own offspring.

Still, hopefully this would be the last

of Johnny's stunts and Jemma could go back to caring for her animals based on science and research.

Then she and Matt could go back to being simply colleagues with no confusing incidents created by Johnny Beckett.

As is often the case when you dread something, Jemma thought, the next morning arrived more quickly than she felt it should. As usual she was at the park early to do all the checks needed before it opened. She had just finished her animal headcount when Rosie bounced into view.

'Jane is going to be here in twenty minutes. Matt wants you to meet him and the film crew in his office. Jane is going to bring Brendan there.'

The baby had a name, which seemed to make it all a bit too real for Jemma. She put a hand out for the nearest chair and tried to take a deep breath. She shook her head. She could do this. All she needed to do was play happy families with Matt for a short while and then it would be over.

The problem was, she knew, not just that she had no experience of babies, but the idea of playing families with Matt. Her imagination had already been doing that and now she was faced with doing it for real, albeit with someone else's baby.

'You'd better go. You don't want to be late,' Rosie said, her eyes gleaming and showing that she was enjoying Jemma's discomfort a little too much. 'Matt's waiting for you.'

Jemma risked a glare.

'Oh, come on, Jemma! He likes you, even you must be able to see that!'

'Rosie, he has a girlfriend.' Jemma hoped that would be the end of it. Even if Rosie didn't think that was an issue in a relationship maybe she could at least accept that for Jemma it was.

'No, he doesn't,' Rosie said, sounding amused.

'Yes, he does. He lives with her and her name is Betty.'

'Betty?' Rosie said reaching out a hand to rest on Jemma's arm. 'Jemma,

Betty is his dog.'

Jemma was sure she had misheard.

'No,' she said slowly, 'Betty is Matt's girlfriend.'

'Did he actually tell you that?' Rosie looked bemused now.

'Well, no,' Jemma said slowly, 'but he talked about her as if . . . '

'As if he was a man who takes good care of his dog?'

'When we had dinner, he said he had to get back to Betty.'

'To let her out, I expect.'

Jemma's mouth formed a perfect 'O' as everything started to make sense. Matt's behaviour and his confusion when she had confronted him. Jemma could feel her cheeks burn as she imagined what Matt must think of her. She spun the chair round and sat down with her head in her hands.

'Are you OK?' Rosie asked, kneeling down and sounding concerned. 'Try taking some slow deep breaths.'

Jemma was definitely not OK. The pieces of the puzzle seemed to be falling into place and left her with a deep sense of burning embarrassment. No wonder he had looked at her as if she was mad. No wonder he had looked confused and hadn't even tried to apologise.

Everything that Jemma thought she knew about Matt was all in her head and that left her with one big problem. How was she going to face him now?

Baby Makes Three

'I can't wait to tell Matt that you thought Betty was his girlfriend. He is going to crease up!' Rosie said, all smiles.

'Rosie, you can't tell him!' Jemma said and knew she sounded desperate. Rosie seemed oblivious to Jemma's trauma and just kept grinning.

'Oh, come on, Jemma, it hilarious. Matt will see the funny side. He's that kind of guy.' Rosie patted Jemma on the shoulder.

Jemma shook her head and tried to take some deep breaths. Rosie looked slightly less amused now and a little concerned, too.

'OK, I won't tell him, if you don't want me to. If you're that worried maybe you should tell him yourself?' Rosie added. 'He might even figure it out himself and that would probably be worse,' she added thoughtfully.

Jemma got to her feet. Listening to Rosie's advice was not helping and a quick glance at her watch told her she would need to jog to get to the office on time.

The walk to the office seemed both the shortest and longest of Jemma's life. She wasn't sure she was ready to see Matt but a part of her was desperate to see him. It was all very confusing, and she didn't know what to do.

As the management suite building came into view, Jemma knew she had a decision to make. She was going to pretend like nothing had happened, like she hadn't accused Matt, in a round-about way, of cheating on his girlfriend or assumed that he had a girlfriend at home. No, she was just going to act like none of that had happened and hope for the best.

Jemma pulled open the door and Johnny and Matt were standing in the reception area. Matt was holding baby Brendan, who was lying in his arms and gazing up at him. Matt seemed as taken with the baby as the baby was with him.

Jemma stopped and allowed herself a few moments to take in the scene. She felt as if someone had reached in to her most personal dreams and plucked out one of the moments and made it real.

'Ah, Jemma, there you are,' Matt said, finally glancing up. 'Would you like to carry Brendan?' Matt was smiling at her and Jemma smiled back.

'He looks comfortable. Why don't you keep hold of him and I'll take that?' Jemma said, indicating the baby bag, which Matt handed over.

'Right, now everyone is here,' Johnny said, giving Jemma a look. Jemma glanced up at the clock on the wall. She knew she wasn't late. The cheek of the man! And she was taking valuable time out of her working day to play at happy families!

Jemma wanted to say something but one look at Matt made her hold her tongue. She just needed to get through this and then she would have done all she had been asked to do.

Johnny pushed past Jemma and walked out of the door.

'After you,' Jemma said, holding the door for Matt, who had his hands full.

They walked together, side by side, through the park towards the panda enclosure. Other visitors glanced their way and Jemma was sure that if she stopped and asked them, they would assume that she and Matt were together, and that Brendan was their baby.

Jemma had never been one hundred percent sure about having her own children and had put that down to not finding the right man to have the children with. Now, walking beside Matt and Brendan, Jemma knew that she had been right. She did want children. The desire seemed to rise inside her as her imagination started to create the picture.

She risked a glance at Matt. Her heart was telling her that she had found the right man but her head was warning caution. She had thought she had felt that way before and that had ended in heartbreak because the man hadn't felt the same.

What if this situation was no different? What if Matt didn't feel anything for her? Could she take the risk and put her feelings out there and ask? She shook her head, sure that she would never be able to get the words out.

'Ah, I think we may need a quick nappy change,' Matt said.

'Are you sure?' Jemma asked. She might deal with cleaning up after animals every day, but babies seemed a whole different ball game. She held her breath, waiting for him to pass the baby to her, sure that he would assume she was more qualified for the job.

'Hand me the bag and I'll do it,' Matt said, still grinning.

Jemma handed him the bag and watched him walk to the nearby baby changing room. As he disappeared into the changing room, Jemma shook her head and tried to decide what she was going to do next.

She needed to find some time to talk

to Matt. Maybe if she explained to him how she had got the wrong end of the stick, he would laugh and tell her that he loved her too. Jemma clenched her fists. Enough dreaming, she told herself. You need to be realistic. He's just as likely to look at you like you are slightly mad and take a few steps backwards for safety.

The door to the changing room opened and Jemma plastered a smile on her face. They needed to get through whatever Johnny had cooked up this time and then perhaps she could suggest that she and Matt go out for a drink. Maybe she could suggest it as some kind of debrief post filming?

Matt was smiling at Brendan and Jemma wondered if Rosie was right and seeing Matt behaving like the perfect dad would be good for the pandas. Jemma laughed out loud. She really was losing the plot if she thought that was true.

Matt looked at her curiously but didn't comment on the fact that she appeared to be laughing at nothing.

'Shall we head to the pandas?' Jemma asked, hoping to shift Matt's attention before he asked for an explanation. 'I think Brendan is up for it if you are.'

As if on cue, Brendan gurgled and clapped his hands. Matt and Jemma both laughed and headed off in the direction of the panda enclosure.

Johnny was waiting for them and tapping his foot impatiently as if they were late for an important appointment.

'Sorry,' Matt said, looking suitably apologetic, 'Brendan needed a quick change but here we are. What do you want us to do?'

'No worries, Mattie boy,' Johnny said with a wide grin. Jemma was sure if she had offered the excuse, Johnny would have glowered at her. 'And action!' Johnny said, pointing a finger at Matt.

Matt nodded slowly, and he seemed as unsure as Jemma was, as to what they were supposed to do now.

'Right, well, let's show Brendan the pandas,' Matt said, walking towards the edge of the enclosure.

Jemma wasn't sure that Brendan would know what he was looking at and even if he did, whether he would be all that enthusiastic, but followed Matt all the same.

'Look, Brendan, pandas!' Matt said and shifted Brendan in his arms so that he was facing outwards and looking towards the pandas.

Jemma looked into the enclosure and could see that both pandas were sound asleep.

Johnny seemed supremely unconcerned by the fact his latest stunt was not having any effect on the pandas. He seemed much more interested in what Matt and Jemma were doing and silently he indicated to Brett to zoom in for a close-up.

Jemma turned to look at Matt and Brendan. Brendan was now chewing on his fist and looking bored, but it wasn't like there was much for him to look at.

'You take him,' Johnny demanded.

Jemma looked at Brendan who

seemed quite content where he was and wondered if she could suggest that he stay with Matt.

Johnny fixed Jemma with a glare and she found herself facing Matt as he handed over Brendan. Jemma tried to remember all that her friend had told her about holding the baby. Matt had made it look so easy but in Jemma's arms, Brendan looked awkward and uncomfortable.

Jemma tried out a smile on Brendan as she saw his bottom lip start to wobble. She shook her head at herself, she just didn't have the knack, not like Matt did.

Brendan threw back his head and let out an ear-splitting wail. Jemma was pretty sure that, wherever Jane was in the park, she would be able to hear it and no doubt come running, wondering what on earth had upset her baby son.

Heartache Ahead?

'Try shifting him round,' Matt suggested and when Jemma looked at him, her expression both panicked and bewildered, Matt reached across and lifted Brendan out of her arms. The wailing stopped as soon as Matt had taken hold of Brendan.

'Now hold your arms like this,' Matt suggested, and Jemma did her best to copy his moves. Matt handed Brendan back to her and she had to agree that it was more comfortable for her, and no doubt Brendan, since the ear-splitting shrieking hadn't restarted.

'You're a natural,' Matt said and there was something about the look on his face that made Jemma's heart beat faster and dots dance in front of her eyes.

'I think you're mistaken,' Jemma managed to say.

'I have three older sisters and they all have children,' Matt said, smoothing down Brendan's fine hair that had been picked up by a light breeze. 'And they all seemed to think that I needed plenty of opportunities to babysit, to prepare me for when I have my own.'

Jemma could feel Matt's eyes on her, but she was almost afraid to look up at him.

She was sure there was a message in what Matt was saying but what if she was wrong? She had been wrong about a lot of things since she had met him.

And besides, talking about the children they might have at some point in the future was moving everything along rather quickly, wasn't it?

'Look!' Johnny said and pointed in the direction of the pandas. Bojing had not only woken up but toddled his way over to the edge of the enclosure and looked, to all intents and purposes, as if he were fascinated by baby Brendan.

Since Bojing was now up close to the glass screen around the enclosure,

Jemma crouched down and held Brendan at panda level. Brendan squealed and held out his hand to the glass. Bojing sniffed at it from his side of the glass and then licked the spot where Brendan's hand was.

Jemma had a very practical view of animals but at the same time she believed they had feelings, just like humans. Bojing tilted his head on one side and looked from Brendan to Jemma. Jemma smiled and looked Bojing in the eye and was sure, perhaps for the first time, that there was more to this panda than his appetite and clumsiness.

When Bojing held out both arms, it looked as if he wanted to hold Brendan and all Jemma could do was hope that he would be the proud father of his own cub some time soon.

In the background there was a grumbling growl and Bojing turned to look around him. Lijuan did not look happy at being deserted mid sleep and was not going to keep quiet about it.

If Jemma hadn't known better she

would have been sure that Bojing shrugged at her as if to say, 'The missus is after me', and she watched as Bojing lumbered back to Lijuan's side.

Brendan seemed unimpressed that his furry playmate had disappeared and yawned widely. Jemma stood back up and felt Matt come to stand beside her.

'That was amazing,' Matt said quietly, his voice full of awe. 'Did you see how he reacted to the baby? You can tell he wants a cub of his own.'

Jemma was going to point out that all mammals had the same instinct around young, that it was evolution and biology rather than an emotional feeling, but in that moment, she wasn't sure that science was right.

She had seen in Bojing exactly what Matt had described and it was, as he said, amazing. So all she did was smile and she was rewarded by Matt smiling back at her, in a way that made her knees feel weak.

The moment was gone when Johnny bounced over.

'Brilliant! Amazing! Couldn't have asked for better footage if I had choreographed it myself!' Johnny said, thumping Matt on the back. 'You were brilliant.'

Matt held out a hand.

'Thank you for all your hard work with the documentary. It will mean a lot to the park and our animals,' he said as Johnny grabbed the offered hand and shook it vigorously.

'Right, I'm off. We've got some last minute background shots to do and then we should be out of your hair,' Johnny said turning his attention back to his crew.

Jemma and Matt watched him and his overly laden film crew stride off.

'I was thinking we should have some sort of wrap party? I think that's what these TV types call it. You know, to celebrate the end of filming and all that. I might even ask Johnny if he has some footage he could show us?'

Jemma wanted to go out to dinner and celebrate but she had been hoping it would be just her and Matt. But still, if she agreed, maybe they would have a chance to talk and she could tell Matt how she felt?

Brendan's head settled on her chest and he gave another impressive yawn, as his eyes fluttered, and he fell asleep. Because it would be worth the risk, wouldn't it?

The worse thing he could say was that he didn't feel the same, and although that sent a cold shiver through Jemma, she knew there was a flip side. What if he did feel the same? What if he loved her as she loved him? What if he was just waiting for her to speak up? What if they had a future together?

'Sounds like a good plan, but do you think the crew will be up for it?'

'I'm sure I can persuade them,' Matt said with a grin. 'I'll ask the rest of the team. I know it's too soon to find out if a cub is on the way, but I think we can all agree that we've made real progress with the pandas and in my book that's worth celebrating.

'I'd best be getting back to work,' he

added, looking at his watch, 'and I told Jane that I'd have Brendan back by two. Do you want me to take him?'

Jemma could feel Matt gaze at her, cradling Brendan in her arms, as he slept peacefully.

'I'll take him. Seems a shame to wake him up,' Jemma said. That was true but she was also reluctant to let go of the baby just yet. Holding him in her arms, once she had found the right position, was more enjoyable than she had imagined.

He smelled of talcum powder and she could feel his chest rise and fall. It felt right somehow and as if a part of her had woken up and she knew that she wanted to one day hold her own baby in her arms.

'He certainly seems content. I said we'd meet Jane in the restaurant. Do you want me to walk with you?' Matt asked.

Jemma smiled. Perhaps she wasn't the only one who didn't want to break up the family group just yet.

'If you aren't too busy?'

Matt shrugged as if it didn't matter.

'Nothing that can't wait,' he said, holding out an arm to the path that would take them up to the restaurant.

They walked side by side and once again Jemma felt like the other visitors would assume that they were together, that Brendan was their baby. She enjoyed the sensation.

★   ★   ★

Matt had sent a message via Rosie that the wrap party would be held at the local pub and everyone was invited. Jemma managed to leave work on time, which meant she had plenty of time to get ready.

Her stomach fizzed with excitement. It was a strange sensation; partly, she thought, because the filming was done and that would mean life at the park could go back to some form of normal; partly because she had the feeling that a panda cub might well be in the park's future; and partly because she was hoping she might get an opportunity to speak to Matt.

Jemma jumped in the shower and then went to cast a critical eye over her wardrobe. She wanted to make an effort without looking like she was making an effort. The sort of thing she had never really mastered.

Looking at her wardrobe, her choices were limited and so she settled on a flowing summer dress that reached her ankles. She cast an assessing eye at herself in the mirror and wondered if she was getting all worked up for nothing.

There was no guarantee that she would have the opportunity to speak to Matt on his own and even if she did, what if he didn't feel the same?

Jemma swallowed. One thing was for sure, she would never know unless she was prepared to risk the heartache of rejection.

Public Humiliation

The party from the wildlife park had taken over the long bar garden. It ran down to fields at the back, which came complete with ponies who were always hanging around waiting to be petted or to be given the odd carrot.

They were in luck, since all the park workers were animal lovers, and when Jemma arrived she could see a gaggle of them at the back of the garden, fussing the ponies and feeding them from a bag which contained carrots and apples.

Jemma glanced at her watch and took a sip of her orange juice. She had decided to stay off the alcohol, so that she could stay focused on her goal. She gazed around in what she hoped would be interpreted as a relaxed manner, but scanning the small crowd for signs of Matt.

When she realised there was no sign

of him she decided to head over and say hello to Rosie and the small group of other park keepers.

'Evening,' Jemma said, 'has everyone got a drink?' Everyone raised their glasses, and a few were nearly empty. 'Any top-ups?' Jemma asked with a smile and then went to the bar with their orders.

When she made her way back to the beer garden with a tray of drinks, the crowd in the beer garden seemed to have swelled in the time she was away and so she had to pick her way past people back to Rosie's group.

Jemma handed out the drinks, but Rosie was nowhere to be seen.

'Anyone seen Rosie?' Jemma asked as she picked up her orange juice and took a sip.

'She's over there with her boyfriend,' Ted said, nodding in the direction of a group of people and Jemma could see that Rosie had her arm wrapped around the waist of Brett, and judging by how he looked down at her, he at least was smitten, and Jemma couldn't help a smile. Rosie made the romance thing look so easy.

Rosie didn't tie herself up in knots, get the wrong idea and then agonise over telling the person she loved how she felt. Perhaps she should ask Rosie's advice? The thought was squashed almost as soon as it occurred.

Rosie might take it upon herself to get involved and that would only make it more mortifying, like being a teenager and getting your best friend to approach your crush for you. No, Jemma was on her own and needed to just do it.

'I'm going to go and see if I can find Johnny,' Jemma said to Ted and his mates. Jemma skirted around the groups, pretending to look for Johnny. She was of course looking for Matt, but it was a good cover story.

It looked to Jemma as if the entire staff from the park had turned out for the wrap party. She wondered if they all just fancied a drink or if they didn't want to miss whatever stunt Johnny might pull next. Or maybe they were all hoping to get a peek at the documentary before it aired?

The thought made her shiver a little. It had been awkward to film and she couldn't imagine how it would feel to see herself on screen. But she was on a mission and nothing was going to get in her way.

Jemma continued her slow circuit of the beer garden and then spotted a couple in close conversation — or was it more than that?

Jemma moved forward so that she could get a closer look and could see that it was the woman who had done the make-up, or Matt's at least, during their initial interview. Jemma took a step sideways and could see who she was talking to. She should have known, she should have recognised the familiar figure, but she hadn't wanted to believe it.

Jemma stopped in her tracks. She didn't want to get caught staring but at the same time she needed to know if it was just a friendly chat about the documentary or if it was something more. The make-up lady flung an arm around Matt's waist and leaned in to whisper something in his ear.

Jemma couldn't hear what the woman had said but Matt's peal of laughter was all she needed to know. All Jemma wanted to do in that moment was run away but made herself walk slowly away as if she was admiring the view of the fields behind the garden.

Jemma had made it far enough away that the other groups were drowning out Matt's laughter and Jemma felt herself relax a little. At least she had saved herself public embarrassment and the shame of telling Matt how she felt, when he clearly didn't feel the same.

She closed her eyes to give herself a minute to compose herself and also to think about some excuse as to why she needed to leave the party early. The sort of excuse that would be easily believable but when she opened her eyes a figure was standing in front of her.

'You should fight for him,' Johnny

said, and Jemma took a big step backwards.

'I ... I don't know what you're talking about ... ' Jemma said, her voice going up a notch as she saw that Johnny had his mobile phone in his hand and was using it like a camera.

'You can't give up, love. I've seen the way you look at him. I've been in this business long enough to recognise the real thing and you,' he said pointing at her with a finger on his free hand, 'have got it bad.'

'Mr Beckett,' Jemma said, feeling that using his title might get her message across, 'I agreed to take part in your 'film' and I have done everything asked of me. But I must ask you now to keep your comments about my private life to yourself.'

Johnny looked at her, his head cocked on one side.

'Suit yourself — but everybody's going to see it, when I show the rough cuts later.' He shrugged as if it made no difference to him, one way or the other.

Jemma felt panic rise up inside her and all she wanted to do was run but it seemed like her legs were in shock and unable to move.

'Film's ready, boss,' Brett said, appearing at Johnny's side and behind him Jemma could see that a projector screen had been put up on the back wall of the pub. Jemma's eyes went wide.

'Don't say I didn't warn you,' Johnny said before handing his mobile over to Brett and whispering something in his ear. Brett stared at Jemma and nodded his head, although he didn't seem that convinced by whatever Johnny had just asked him to do.

'If I can have everyone's attention!' Johnny yelled and the crowd of guests stopped talking and turned their attention to him.

'My crew and I would like to thank Matt for this generous wrap party.'

A cheer rippled around the crowd.

'And in return we would like to show you a little film that we put together of our time here at the zoo with you.'

Johnny beamed at the assembled guests, his eyes twinkling.

Jemma knew that Brett was filming her on Johnny's mobile phone but she couldn't tear her eyes away from the movie that was showing.

There were a few clips of various staff saying the wrong thing and a few animal out-takes but the majority of it seemed to focus on her and Matt. Or should that be her reaction to Matt.

The film had been cut in such a way that she came across as a love-struck teenager. The crowd fell silent and Jemma knew that all eyes were on her.

Jemma looked down at her feet and started to walk towards the gate that led to the pub car park. She couldn't turn around. If she did, everyone would see her crying.

Tangled Web

Jemma had finally cried herself to sleep. To have a crush on someone who obviously didn't feel the same was one thing, but to have to share it so publicly with everyone she worked with, was another.

There had been too many days lately that she had had to put a brave face on it and show up at work as if nothing had happened. But today, she knew she didn't have it in her.

She also knew that if she didn't go in to work today, it would likely only make it harder to go in the day after, but today she didn't care. She had never called in sick for anything other than an illness which had confined her to bed.

Jemma was still in bed, of course, but today it was because she was emotionally worn out rather than physically unable. Today, for the first day in her life, she was going to stay in bed and feel sorry for herself.

She picked up her phone and sent Rosie a text. Protocol was to call in to the main office but there was no way she was up for that. For one thing, half the office staff had been at the farewell party and for another Jemma wasn't sure she would be able to speak.

Every time she thought about trying, her throat closed up and fresh tears fell. It was like what had happened with George all over again, except this time she was going to give in to how she was feeling and allow herself some time to wallow.

Mid-morning, Jemma padded out to her kitchen and put the kettle on before reaching into the top cupboard for her emergency supply of expensive hot chocolate. In the cupboard she also found marshmallows and a can of whipped cream. Today she was going all out.

As the kettle boiled she reached in the freezer for a tub of ice cream and found a teaspoon on the kitchen drainer. Jemma had made a surprisingly big dent in it by the time her hot chocolate was cool enough to drink.

She was just making her way back to bed, with her mug in one hand and the tub in the other when there was a knock at her door. Jemma kept shuffling towards her bedroom. There was no way she was opening the door. It was probably just the gas man or the postman, and either of them would leave a card and she could sort the reading, or parcel pick up, later.

Jemma put her mug on the coaster on her bedside table when the knocking started again. She frowned, wondering if perhaps it was Rosie who had come to see how she was.

Rosie probably wouldn't go away until she answered and so with much rolling of eyes, she pulled on her fluffy dressing-gown and staggered back down the stairs to the front door. Taking a deep breath, she opened the door and promptly closed it again.

'I don't want to talk to you,' Jemma said through the closed door but sure that Matt could hear her.

'You don't need to talk, you just need to listen,' Matt said. He had now lifted the letter box up so his voice carried better.

'I know what you're going to say,' Jemma said, 'so I'll save us both the embarrassment and tell you, you don't need to say anything. I understand.' Jemma could feel tears building up behind her eyes and she rubbed at them fiercely. She did not want to cry in front of Matt, even if he couldn't actually see her.

'Jemma, I came here to say what I needed to say. I can either stand on your doorstep and say it or you can invite me in and I can stop drawing the attention of your neighbours.'

Jemma glared at the door. Why couldn't he just leave? It seemed like everything in her life was about embarrassing her!

'Seriously, Jemma, I think the man next door is going to call the police.'

Jemma stared at the floor. Mr Jenkins

was lovely and quite protective of her in a grandfatherly way and so he probably would call the police.

'Fine,' Jemma said and pulled the door open. 'Come in and say what you want to but then I need you to leave.'

Jemma turned her back on Matt and the door and walked into the living-room, hoping that those couple of extra seconds would give her the time to find a neutral expression and some inner calm.

Matt was going to apologise, say that he was sorry she had got the wrong idea and then Jemma could point out that technically it was Johnny that had got the wrong idea.

He was, after all, the one who had told Jemma that Matt had feelings for her, too. Not that she was going to tell Matt that, but she was going to tell him that she understood he was now with the make-up lady. She didn't want to lie about how she felt but she didn't want to tell Matt, either. That wouldn't help either of them.

Jemma wrapped her dressing-gown

around her before settling herself in the armchair near the open fire. This meant Matt couldn't sit next to her and instead had to choose either the other wooden rocking chair or the two-seater sofa. He chose the sofa.

'I'm sorry to disturb you when you aren't well,' Matt said, and he did look suitably apologetic.

'It's just a headache,' Jemma said which was half true since she could feel one starting up behind her right eye. Matt nodded and then looked at his feet and Jemma felt like ice had dropped into her stomach.

'Is it one of the animals?' She shook her head at herself. She was so wrapped up in her own misery that she hadn't given a thought as to whether Matt had come to see her about something else, something bad. She clenched her hands in her lap. She should have gone in to work.

'Jemma, the animals are all fine. I'm sorry — I should have made that clear.'

The clamp that seemed to have

formed around Jemma's chest loosened slightly. She knew she would eventually recover from her broken heart.

She had done it before and she could do it again, but she didn't think she could forgive herself it something happened to one of her animals because she had taken the day off to wallow in self-pity.

'Good, that's good.' The relief was real, but Jemma knew that she still needed to sit and listen to Matt apologise, maybe for not feeling the same way that she did. It would all be uncomfortable and embarrassing, but they might as well get on with it.

'So, what did you want to say?' Jemma asked, lifting a hand to her forehead and rubbing at it, hoping that Matt might remember that she had said she had a headache and talk quickly.

'Sorry yes, I won't keep you. I expect you want to lie down in the quiet. It's just, after last night, I knew I needed to come and talk to you.'

Jemma couldn't wait any longer.

'Matt, its fine. Johnny has been saying outrageous things since he arrived and clearly cut the film together to make a point. But filming has finished and so we can all go back to life as normal.'

'It is about the film,' Matt said slowly, as if he were trying to work out what the right words were, 'and also about Jen and me.'

'I hope you'll be very happy together,' Jemma blurted out. She hadn't meant to say that, but it was the first thing that came to mind.

'That's just it. We aren't together.'

Jemma raised a sceptical eyebrow.

'I'm not sure what it is with us two, but we always seem to be getting the wrong idea about each other.'

Jemma could feel a tiny bubble of anger break through the pain.

'I'm not sure how I've given you the wrong idea, Matt, but you and Jen seemed to be the perfect couple last night.'

'Jen and I are just friends,' Matt said carefully. Jemma thought privately that he had never behaved like that with her, but maybe he didn't consider them as friends.

'And you know that Betty is my dog, right?'

Jemma was so glad that Rosie had explained this to her, or this moment might be even more mortifying.

'Yes, I'm aware of that.'

'Because for a while there you were acting like she was my girlfriend.' Again, Matt was speaking carefully, and Jemma could feel that he was searching her face for her reaction. The blush started at her neck and rose up her face and so she knew there would be no chance of bluffing her way out of this one.

'It's true that I did think that she was. For a time.'

'Which is why you reacted like you did at the dance,' Matt said, looking as if things were starting to make more sense.

'I just felt like you might have been being disloyal,' Jemma said, looking anywhere but at Matt.

'Right,' he said, and Jemma thought

she had insulted him again.

'I didn't mean that I expected you to behave like that, it's just . . . ' Jemma's voice trailed away as she felt like she was digging herself into a hole. She looked up sharply when she realised that Matt was in fact laughing.

'You must have thought I was a total rat,' he said, wiping at his eyes.

'Well, can you blame me?' Jemma said a little huffily.

'Not at all. It's just all starting to make sense.'

They sat and looked at each other and Jemma wasn't quite sure what was going on.

'OK,' Matt said, 'just so we are clear. Betty is my dog, whom I adore, and I have a camera at home that she can activate and when she does it sends a message to my phone.' He pulled his phone out of his pocket and waved it at her. 'Then I can talk to her over the video and I even have a treat dispenser. If I tap the app on my phone it gives her a treat.'

Jemma nodded slowly, thinking that Matt was starting to make a bit more sense to her, too.

'I don't normally tell people because I worry that they might think I'm a bit weird, you know — overly attached.'

'Probably not something you need to worry about when you are talking to people who care for animals for a living,' Jemma said, and she allowed herself a small smile as Matt looked a little rueful.

'Good point. And then there was your history.'

Jemma sat up straight in her arm-chair.

'My history?' Jemma wasn't sure if she was annoyed that someone had told Matt or worried what he would make of what he had been told.

'I don't know the details,' Matt said holding his hands up to signify surrender. 'I just asked Rosie about . . . ' Matt's voice trailed off as he caught sight of Jemma's expression. 'I wasn't being nosey I just wanted to . . . ' Again, Matt seemed to have lost the power of speech.

Jemma could feel indignation bubble up inside and she was ready to give Matt a piece of her mind and then she saw his face. Matt looked worried and concerned. He wasn't simply defending his actions, as George had done, he seemed genuinely concerned about how she felt.

'I know I'm not the easiest person to figure out.' Jemma knew it was true, for one thing Rosie had told her many times, that she didn't give much away. Matt let out a sigh and he looked relieved.

'I could tell that you had been hurt before and I didn't want to rush anything. And then after the dinner, I thought . . . but then the dance . . . '

Matt didn't really need to fill in the gaps because Jemma knew exactly how he had felt. A one point or other during the time they had known each other she had felt the same but it seemed obvious that they had not felt the same at the same point in time. No wonder they had both been confused by each other's actions!

It was, in fact, a mess. And when that thought occurred to her all she could do was laugh.

Matt looked at her uncertainly and then seeing that Jemma was laughing because she found the whole thing funny, he joined in.

Together at Last

Jemma had offered to make them both a cup of tea, but Matt had spotted the hot chocolate and marshmallows and so Jemma made that instead. Then they returned to her lounge and curled up at each end of the sofa, both cradling their steaming mugs.

'So . . . ' Jemma said. They had established that they had both at various points got the wrong end of the stick but that was about as far as the discussion had gone so far. She wondered if now was the time to be brave.

'So?' Matt said, and Jemma knew that he was waiting for her to say something first.

'So, I admit that throughout all this I have got the wrong idea about some key things.'

Matt nodded. It was clear to Jemma that he wasn't going to help her out and she was in fact, on her own. She took a deep breath and looked him straight in the eye.

'But around all that I have found myself having feelings for you.'

'Feelings?' Matt queried but a smile was tugging at the corner of his lips and so Jemma nudged him with her foot.

'Are you going to let me finish?'

'Of course, my apologies.'

'It has been very confusing.' Jemma mentally rolled her eyes at herself and told herself firmly to get a grip and get on with it. 'What I'm trying to say is that I like you, Matt.' She grimaced at her own inability to say the word. 'No, more than that — I think I love you.'

The words came out in such a rush that Jemma wasn't sure that Matt would be able to understand what she was trying to say.

Matt nodded, as if she were handing over the next month's staff rosters rather than making a declaration of love, and made a show of being lost in thought. Jemma nudged him again and raised her eyebrow.

'Dramatic pausing not helping?' he said with a smile and she gave him a playful glare. 'OK, I get the message. Get on with it, Matthew, something my mother is always saying to me. You'll like her,' he added with a grin, 'and she is going to love you.'

Jemma thought she might burst if Matt didn't get on with it and so she leaned over and kissed him softly on the lips. That seemed to focus his mind and he kissed her back in such a way that Jemma thought she probably knew the answer to the question she was dying to ask.

Matt was the first to pull back but not far, just far enough so that she could see his face clearly.

'I love you, Jemma. I think I have from the moment I first saw you.' He leaned in and kissed her again. 'I'm sorry that I've made everything so confusing and complicated.'

'Me too, although I think most of that is my fault.'

'Well, now you come to mention it ... ' Matt said but Jemma silenced him once again with a kiss, interrupted by the beep of Matt's phone.

'Johnny's heading off to the airport. Apparently his next filming is taking place in Thailand.'

Matt looked at Jemma and grinned.

'So you won't be forced to put on any more performances for the viewing public.'

Jemma tilted her head on one side.

'Don't you think the viewing public have a right to know how the story ends?' She smiled just a little as for the first time she thought she didn't mind one bit that her personal life was going to make it on to the small screen.

'I don't know,' Matt said cautiously. 'Do you?'

'I think if the viewing public have watched the whole documentary they should be first to know the happy news?'

'Lijuan's pregnant?' Matt said excitedly. Jemma gave him the look.

'Oh, *that* news,' he said with a smile.

'I'm sure Johnny will have a camera with him and no doubt he will think that the airport is the perfect romantic setting.'

'I'm up for it if you are but there's just one thing.'

'What?' Jemma couldn't think what would stop them, unless Matt had an important meeting to go to, or something.

'I'm not sure you want to go to the airport, not to mention appearing in a TV documentary, in your fluffy pyjamas, as cute as they are.'

Jemma looked down and squeaked.

'Give me five minutes!' And she rushed out of the room.

★　★　★

Matt's car screeched into short term parking and he drove them around and around the multi-storey as they looked for a space. Jemma couldn't help looking at the clock on the dashboard and hoping that they would make it in time.

Matt put his foot to the floor and pulled into a spot, parking at such an angle that he could only just squeeze himself out of the door. Jemma's door swung wide and she was out and running, with Matt close on her heels. He caught her with ease and she felt him reach for her hand. They ran together through the airport to the departure lounge.

International departures was heaving with people and trolleys and suitcases, some wandering around looking lost and others walking determinedly towards the long row of airline desks.

'I see him, over there!' Matt shouted and tugged at Jemma's hand so that she started to run again. Matt had pointed out a figure who was weaving in and out of the crowds, followed by a small entourage, who were laden down with bags and boxes.

'Johnny!' Matt shouted as the man moved nearer to security and the point at which they wouldn't be able to see him any more. Johnny had his head down, focusing on his phone and seemed oblivious.

'Mr Beckett!' Jemma shouted. She didn't think she could bear to not have the happy ending form part of the documentary.

After the footage from the pub last night, it seemed only right to tell the viewers how the story had ended. At Jemma's shout, Johnny stopped in his tracks and looked about him. Matt and Jemma slid to a stop beside him.

'Mr Beckett!' Jemma said breathlessly. 'I'm so glad we caught you.'

Johnny looked from Jemma to Matt and then down to see their entwined hands and his face broke into a broad grin.

'I knew it! Johnny is never wrong, my girl! You mark my words — you'll be married within the year.'

Jemma could feel herself blush a little. He had been right, of course. She just wasn't entirely sure if Johnny's interference had been a help or a hindrance to their romance. She suspected it had been a real help but she wasn't sure she was ready to tell Johnny that just yet.

Johnny clicked his fingers and started issuing instructions. Cameras were pulled out of cases and pointed in their direction and then Johnny insisted that they re-enact their arrival and the announcement of their news, which Jemma and Matt dutifully did.

Jemma didn't think anything, even the embarrassment of acting at the airport, could take the smile off her face today. When they had acted to Johnny's satisfaction, he clicked his fingers and the crew worked to repack all the equipment.

'Well I'm off to Thailand to shoot a reality TV show about famous people becoming Buddhist monks so I'd best be off. But I'll be back when the baby panda is born.' He grinned.

'Well, that would be lovely, Johnny, but we still don't know if Lijuan is actually . . . ' Jemma was cut off by a wave of Johnny's hand but instead of looking annoyed with her as he usually did, he just grinned more broadly and tapped the side of his nose with one finger.

'I am always right. You should have learned that by now, girlie.' With that, he nodded at them both and turned on his heel before disappearing through the doors to the security check area.

'I hope he is right,' Matt said, pulling Jemma into his arms.

'Me too, it would be amazing to have a panda cub.'

'It would but that wasn't what I was thinking about.'

Jemma looked up at him and he smiled before kissing her as if she had just returned from a trip that had kept them apart for months.

* * *

Matt was the first to speak. They had all been taking it in turns to get some sleep and watch the monitors and Jemma was beginning to wonder if it would ever happen.

'Johnny was right,' Matt said as they all got their first look at the tiny, pink, bald creature that Bojing was licking. After nearly five months of pregnancy, Lijuan had finally had her baby.

'I told you,' Johnny said from his seat next to Jemma and they all laughed softly. No-one wanted to disturb the new parents.

'Well, you were right about us,' Matt said, pulling Jemma to her feet and into his arms. 'Jemma and I are getting married next month.'

'I told you that, too, and to think that if I hadn't stepped in you might still be making puppy eyes at each other from afar.'

Matt and Jemma exchanged looks and then grinned.

'I wanted to get married straight away but Jemma thought that we should wait,' Matt confided.

'I said it wasn't possible to plan a wedding in a week, like you suggested,' Jemma said, nudging him in the ribs. 'Five months has been an amazing feat of organisation.'

'But you're so good at that.' Matt smiled.

'I am but I'm not wonder woman. I don't have magical powers.'

'Oh, I don't know . . . ' Matt said leaning in to kiss Jemma again.

'And besides you want an exotic honeymoon and I couldn't go away until I knew the cub was safely here,' Jemma said.

'And even now I'm sure you'll be checking the video feed every day when you're away,' Rosie said.

'That was what we agreed,' Jemma said with a grin.

'And I'll provide full updates every day on the welfare of all the animals,' Rosie said as if she had been told to do this a thousand times.

'Anything to keep my wife happy,' Matt said, and Jemma felt a surge of joy at the thought of being Mrs Darnell.

'I'm so glad that you could be here to see the panda cub arrive,' Jemma said, turning her attention back to Johnny.

'Well, it was in the contract,' Johnny said as if that it explained it all. Jemma smiled.

'And you're going to be able to extend your stay to come to the wedding?' Jemma asked.

For the first time since Jemma had met him, Johnny actually looked lost for words.

'I would be honoured,' he finally said.

Jemma wriggled out of Matt's arms and walked over to give the TV man a kiss on the cheek.

'Good. It wouldn't be the same without you.'

Jemma wasn't sure, but she thought Johnny was blushing.

'You two will be very happy together.' Johnny said. 'I know it,' he added with a smile.

'Well, you are always right,' Matt said, grinning, before pulling Jemma into his arms and kissing her.

We do hope that you have enjoyed reading this large print book.

Did you know that all of our titles are available for purchase?

We publish a wide range of high quality large print books including:
Romances, Mysteries, Classics
General Fiction
Non Fiction and Westerns

Special interest titles available in large print are:
The Little Oxford Dictionary
Music Book, Song Book
Hymn Book, Service Book

Also available from us courtesy of Oxford University Press:
Young Readers' Dictionary
(large print edition)
Young Readers' Thesaurus
(large print edition)

For further information or a free brochure, please contact us at:
Ulverscroft Large Print Books Ltd.,
The Green, Bradgate Road, Anstey,
Leicester, LE7 7FU, England.
Tel: (00 44) **0116 236 4325**
Fax: (00 44) **0116 234 0205**

Catrin confronts a man trespassing on her Aunt Hazel's land, only to learn that he is Hazel's godson, Alex. He's a successful architect, handsome but irritating — and when he offers to buy Hazel's property, Catrin is immediately suspicious. Can she trust his motives, or does he have something to gain from the arrangement? Accompanying Hazel on a trip to Corsica, Catrin ponders this — but when Alex turns up unexpectedly, her feelings begin to change. Still, she's determined to uncover his true intentions for her aunt's land . . .